THE DROWNED WORLD

THE DROWNED

WORLD

J.G. BALLARD

WITH AN INTRODUCTION BY MARTIN AMIS

LIVERIGHT PUBLISHING CORPORATION
A DIVISION OF W. W. NORTON & COMPANY
NEW YORK · LONDON

For information about permission to reproduce selections from this book,
write to Permissions, Liveright Publishing Corporation,
500 Fifth Avenue, New York, NY 10110

For information about special discounts for bulk purchases, please contact
W. W. Norton Special Sales at specialsales@wwnorton.com or 800-233-4830

Manufacturing by LSC Harrisonburg
Book design by Chris Welch
Production manager: Louise Mattarelliano

Library of Congress Cataloging-in-Publication Data

Ballard, J. G., 1930–2009.
The drowned world / J.G. Ballard , introduction by Martin Amis.
p. cm.
ISBN 978-0-87140-406-0 (hardcover)
I. Title.
PR6052.A46D76 2012
823'.914—dc23
2011050207

ISBN 978-0-87140-362-9 pbk.

Liveright Publishing Corporation
500 Fifth Avenue, New York, N.Y. 10110
www.wwnorton.com

W. W. Norton & Company Ltd.
15 Carlisle Street, London W1D 3BS

6 7 8 9 0

CONTENTS

Contents

INTRODUCTION
Martin Amis

Is prescience a literary virtue? And should the work of J.G. Ballard be particularly prized (as some critics maintain) for the 'uncanny' accuracy of its forecasts? The answer to both these questions, I suggest, is a cheerful no.

In *The Atrocity Exhibition* (1970) Ballard famously tapped Ronald Reagan for president. His *Hello America* (1981), on the other hand, surmised that the United States in its entirety would be evacuated by 1990. The meteorological cataclysms envisaged by his first four novels still look plausible. But the social crisis envisaged by his last four novels—violent and widespread anomie brought about by a glut of leisure and wealth—now looks vanishingly remote.

So here's a prophecy: fictional divination will always be hopelessly haphazard. The unfolding of world historical events is itself haphazard (and therefore unaesthetic), and 'the future' is in a sense defined by its messy inscrutability. Besides, the art of fiction owes allegiance to a muse, a goddess as pure as her nine sisters, and not to some bustling Madame Sosostris (Eliot's 'famous clairvoyant', with her 'wicked pack of cards'). Nevertheless there are certain writers whose visionary power is indifferent to the corroboration of mere upshots—writers who seem to be able to feel, and use, the 'world hum' of the 'near-after'. That first quote is from Don DeLillo, who is one such; the second quote is from James Graham Ballard (1930–2009), who is another.

Ballard foresaw manmade climate change, not in *The Drowned World* (1962), but in *The Drought* (1964). In *The Drought* (originally entitled *The Burning World*), industrial waste has thickened the mantle of the oceans and destroyed the precipitation cycle, transforming the planet into a wilderness of dust and fire. In *The Drowned World*, ecological catastrophe has a quite different set of causes. The median temperature at the Equator is one hundred and eighty degrees and rising, the polar ice caps and the permafrost have melted, Europe is 'a system of giant lagoons', the American Midwest is 'an enormous gulf opening into the Hudson Bay', and the global population (down to five million) huddles within the Arctic and Antarctic Circles (where the thermometers, for now, record a 'pleasant' eighty-five). And how did all this come about? Solar instability, pure and simple, with no help whatever from *Homo sapiens*. So, on the basis of this one novel, Ballard could unobtrusively add his voice to the current Republican debate on global warming—slightly to the left of Rick Perry and Michele Bachmann, true, but slightly to the right of Mitt Romney.

This is an irony we need not fear; indeed, it speeds us on our way to more central questions. As a man (and as a good Green), Ballard was naturally on the side of the angels, but as an artist he is unconditionally of the devil's party. He loves the glutinous jungles of *The Drowned World* and the tindery deserts of *The Drought*—just as he loves the super-hurricane, or express avalanche, of *The Wind from Nowhere* (1961) and the mineralised multiplicities of *The Crystal World* (1966). It is the measure of his creative radicalism that he welcomes these desperate dystopias with every atom of his being. When he turned away from hardcore science fiction in the 1950s, Ballard rejected 'outer space' in favour of its opposite: 'inner space'. Accordingly, he merges with his conjured futures, internalising them in a kind of imaginative martyrdom. The fusion of mood and setting, the mapping of a land-scape of the troubled mind—this is what really matters in Ballard. It gives the novels their tight clench of waywardness and fixity.

'Soon it would be too hot' is the laconic first sentence of *The Drowned World*. Its hero, the marine biologist Robert Kerans, is staring out from the balcony of his suite at the Ritz; he is the only (mammalian) occupant of the hotel; the rising water is ten storeys from his feet.

> Even through the massive olive-green fronds the relentless power of the sun was plainly tangible. The blunt refracted rays drummed against his bare chest and shoulders. . . . The solar disc was no longer a well-defined sphere, but a wide expanding ellipse that fanned out across the eastern horizon like a colossal fire-ball, its reflection turning the dead leaden surface of the lagoon into a brilliant copper shield.

The sun is alarmingly distended. It is also alarmingly *noisy*; it 'thuds' and 'booms'; we hear 'the volcanic pounding' of its flares. There are mosquitoes the size of dragonflies, hammer-nosed bats, wolf spiders. There are iguanas and basilisks—at one point a large caiman sees Kerans 'waist-deep among the horse-tails' and veers towards him, 'its eyes steadying' (that 'steadying' is awfully good). The water gives off an unendurable reek, 'the sweet com-pacted smells of dead vegetation and rotting animal carcases'. Kerans watches the 'countless reflections of the sun move across the surface in huge sheets of fire, like the blazing facetted eyes of gigantic insects'. Beneath the lagoon is a city: 'Free of vegetation, apart from a few drifting clumps of Sargasso weed, the streets and shops had been preserved almost intact, like a reflection in a lake that has somehow lost its original'. The city is London.

Kerans is nominally engaged with a team of scientists on a

waterborne testing station, but the work has become pointlessly routine. Fauna and flora are faithfully following 'the emergent lines anticipated twenty years earlier', namely an accelerated counter-evolution, a retrogression into a world of lizards and rain forests under a Triassic sun. The human actors have embarked on a parallel process—within the diameter of their own skulls. Early on we learn that something has gone wrong with *sleep*: at night, the protagonists enter the 'time jungles' of uterine dreams, descending into their amniotic past and also into the past of the species, experiencing the 'archaic memories' (the 'organic memories' of danger and terror) encrypted in their spinal cords. Some fear these dreams. Kerans, of course, embraces them, and yearningly submits to their domination of his waking mind:

> Guided by his dreams, he was moving backwards
> through the emergent past, through a succession of
> ever stranger landscapes, centred upon the lagoon. . . .
> At times the circle of water was spectral and vibrant,
> at others slack and murky, the shore apparently formed
> of shale, like the dull metallic skin of a reptile. Yet
> again the soft beaches would glow invitingly with
> a glossy carmine sheen, the sky warm and limpid,
> the emptiness of the long stretches of sand total and
> absolute, filling him with an exquisite and tender
> anguish.

Ballard gives *The Drowned World* the trappings of a conventional novel (hero, heroine, authority figure, villain) and equips it with a plot (jeopardy, climax, resolution, coda), but all this feels dutiful and perfunctory, as if conventionality simply bores him. Thus the novel's backdrop is boldly futuristic while its mechanics seem antique (with something of the Boy's-Own innocence we find in John Buchan and C. S. Forester). In addition, Ballard's strikingly 'square' dialogue remains a serious lacuna. Here as elsewhere, his dramatis personae—supposedly so gaunt and ghostly—talk like a troupe of British schoolteachers hoisted out of the 1930s: 'Damn' shame about old Bodkin', 'Capital!', 'Touché, Alan'. (Cf. DeLillo, whose dialogue is always fluidly otherworldly.) We conclude that Ballard is quite unstimulated by human interaction—unless it takes the form of something inherently weird, like mob atavism or mass hysteria. What excites him is human isolation.

The 'otherness' of Ballard, his mesmeric glazedness, is always attributed to the two years he spent in a Japanese internment camp in Shanghai (1943–45). That experience, I think, should be seen in combination, or in synergy, with the two years he spent dissecting cadavers as a medical student in Cambridge (1949–51). Again the dichotomy: as a man he was ebulliently social (and humourous), but as an artist he is fiercely solitary (and humourless). The outcome, in any event, is a genius for the perverse and the obsessional, realised in a prose style of hypnotically varied vowel sounds (its diction enriched by a wide range of technical vocabularies). In the end, the tensile strength of *The Drowned World* derives not from its action but from its poetry.

'Soon it would be too hot.' Yes, and soon it will be time to abandon the lagoon and the drowned city; they will evacuate north, to one of the last human redoubts, Camp Byrd, in Arctic Greenland. There are, after all, pressing reasons to go: the mutating mosquitoes and mutating malarias, the new skin cancers caused by the evaporating cloud cover, the increasingly brazen encroachments of the reptiles, the coming of the Equatorial rain belts and the Equatorial heat. Kerans is, inevitably, the last to leave. He does so on foot (on foot singular, with an infected leg wound and a crutch). And which way is he heading, as the novel closes? Even a reader quite new to Ballard will by this stage consent to the logic of it. 'There isn't any other direction.' He is heading south.

—2011

THE DROWNED WORLD

1

ON THE BEACH AT THE RITZ

SOON IT WOULD be too hot. Looking out from the hotel balcony shortly after eight o'clock, Kerans watched the sun rise behind the dense groves of giant gymnosperms crowding over the roofs of the abandoned department stores four hundred yards away on the east side of the lagoon. Even through the massive olive-green fronds the relentless power of the sun was plainly tangible. The blunt refracted rays drummed against his bare chest and shoulders, drawing out the first sweat, and he put on a pair of heavy sunglasses to protect his eyes. The solar disc was no longer a well-defined sphere, but a wide expanding ellipse that fanned out across the eastern horizon like a colossal fire-ball, its reflection turning the dead leaden surface of the lagoon into a brilliant copper shield. By noon, less than four hours away, the water would seem to burn.

Usually Kerans woke at five, and reached the biological testing station in time to do at least four or five hours' work before the heat became intolerable, but this morning he found himself reluctant to leave the cool, air-curtained haven of the hotel suite. He had spent a couple of hours over breakfast alone, and then completed a six-page entry in his diary, deliberately delaying his departure until Colonel Riggs passed the hotel in his patrol boat, knowing that by then it would be too late to go to the station. The Colonel was always eager for an hour of conversation, particularly when sustained by a few rounds of aperitif, and it would be at least eleven-thirty before he left, his thoughts solely upon lunch at the base.

For some reason, however, Riggs had been delayed. Presumably he was carrying out a longer sweep than usual of the adjacent lagoons, or perhaps was waiting for Kerans to arrive at the testing station. For a moment Kerans wondered whether to try to reach him on the radio transmitter installed by the signals unit in the lounge, but the console was buried under a pile of books, its battery flat. The corporal in charge of the radio station at the base had protested to Riggs when his cheerful morning round-up of old pop songs and local news—an attack by two iguanas on the helicopter the previous night, the latest temperature and humidity readings—had been cut off abruptly half-way through the first instalment. But Riggs recognized Kerans' unconscious attempt to sever his links with the base—the careful haphazardness of the pyramid of books hiding the set contrasted too obviously with Kerans' otherwise meticulous neatness—and tolerantly accepted his need to isolate himself.

LEANING ON THE BALCONY RAIL, the slack water ten storeys below reflecting his thin angular shoulders and gaunt profile, Kerans watched one of the countless thermal storms rip through a clump of huge horse-tails lining the creek which led out of the lagoon. Trapped by the surrounding buildings and the inversion layers a hundred feet above the water, pockets of air would heat rapidly, then explode upwards like escaping balloons, leaving behind them a sudden detonating vacuum. For a few seconds the steam clouds hanging over the creek dispersed, and a vicious miniature tornado lashed across the 60-feet-high plants, toppling them like matchsticks. Then, as abruptly, the storm vanished and the great columnar trunks subsided among one another in the water like sluggish alligators.

Rationalising, Kerans told himself that he had been wise to remain in the hotel—the storms were erupting more and more frequently as the temperature rose—but he knew that his real motive was his acceptance that little now remained to be done. The biological mapping had become a pointless game, the new flora following exactly the emergent lines anticipated twenty years earlier, and he was sure that no one at Camp Byrd in Northern Greenland bothered to file his reports, let alone read them.

In fact, old Dr. Bodkin, Kerans' assistant at the station, had slyly prepared what purported to be an eye-witness description by one of Colonel Riggs' sergeants of a large sail-backed lizard with a gigantic dorsal fin which had been seen cruising across one of the lagoons, in all respects indistinguishable from the Pelycosaur, an early Pennsylvanian reptile. Had the report been taken at its face value—heralding the momentous return of the age of the great reptiles—an army of ecologists would have descended on them immediately, backed by a tactical atomic weapons unit and orders to proceed south at a steady twenty knots. But apart from the routine acknowledgement signal nothing had been heard. Perhaps the specialists at Camp Byrd were too tired even to laugh.

AT THE END of the month Colonel Riggs and his small holding unit would complete their survey of the city (had it once been Berlin, Paris or London?, Kerans asked himself) and set off northward, towing the testing station with them. Kerans found it difficult to believe that he would ever leave the penthouse suite where he had lived for the past six months. The Ritz's reputation, he gladly agreed, was richly deserved—the bathroom, for example, with its black marble basins and gold-plated taps and mirrors, was like the side-chapel of a cathedral. In a curious way it satisfied him to think that he was the last guest who would stay at the hotel, identifying what he realized was a concluding phase of his own life—the northward odyssey through the drowned cities in the south, soon to end with their return to Camp Byrd and its bracing disciplines—and this farewell sunset of the hotel's long splendid history.

He had commandeered the Ritz the day after their arrival, eager to exchange his cramped cabin among the laboratory benches at the testing station for the huge, high-ceilinged state-rooms of the deserted hotel. Already he accepted the lavish brocaded furniture and the bronze art nouveau statuary in the corridor niches as a natural background to his existence, savouring the subtle atmosphere of melancholy that surrounded these last vestiges of a level of civilization now virtually vanished forever. Too many of the other buildings around the lagoon had long since slipped and slid away below the silt, revealing their gimcrack origins, and the Ritz now stood in splendid isolation on the west shore, even the rich blue moulds sprouting from the carpets in the dark corridors adding to its 19th-century dignity.

The suite had originally been designed for a Milanese financier, and was lavishly furnished and engineered. The heat curtains were still perfectly sealed, although the first six storeys of the hotel were below water-level and the load walls were beginning to crack, and the 250-amp. air-conditioning unit had worked without a halt. Although it had been unoccupied for ten years little dust had collected over the mantelpieces and gilt end-tables, and the triptych of photographic portraits on the crocodile-skin desk—financier, financier and sleek well-fed family, financier and even sleeker fifty-storey office block—revealed scarcely a blemish. Luckily for Kerans, his predecessor had left in a hurry, and the cupboards and wardrobes were packed with treasure, ivory-handled squash rackets and hand-printed dressing gowns, the cocktail bar stocked with an ample supply of what were now vintage whiskies and brandies.

————

A GIANT ANOPHELES MOSQUITO, the size of a dragon-fly, spat through the air past his face, then dived down towards the floating jetty where Kerans' catamaran was moored. The sun was still hidden behind the vegetation on the eastern side of the lagoon, but the mounting heat was bringing the huge predatory insects out of their lairs all over the moss-covered surface of the hotel. Kerans was reluctant to leave the balcony and retreat behind the wire-mesh enclosure. In the early morning light a strange mournful beauty hung over the lagoon; the somber green-black fronds of the gymnosperms, intruders from the Triassic past, and the half-submerged white-faced buildings of the 20th century still reflected together in the dark mirror of the water, the two interlocking worlds apparently suspended at some junction in time, the illusion momentarily broken when a giant water-spider cleft the oily surface a hundred yards away.

In the distance, somewhere beyond the drowned bulk of a large Gothic building half a mile to the south, a diesel engine coughed and surged. Kerans left the balcony, closing the wire door behind him, and went into the bathroom to shave. Water had long ceased to flow through the taps, but Kerans maintained a reservoir in the plunge bath, carefully purified in a home-made still on the roof and piped in through the window.

Although he was only forty, Kerans' beard had been turned white by the radio-fluorine in the water, but his bleached crew-cut hair and deep amber tan made him appear at least ten years younger. A chronic lack of appetite, and the new malarias, had shrunk the dry leathery skin under his cheekbones, emphasizing the ascetic cast of his face. As he shaved he examined his features critically, feeling the narrowing planes with his fingers, kneading the altered musculature which was slowly transforming its contours and revealing a personality that had remained latent during his previous adult life. Despite his introspective manner, he now seemed more relaxed and equable than he could remember, his cool blue eyes surveying himself with ironic detachment.

The slightly self-conscious absorption in his own world, with its private rituals and observances, had passed. If he kept himself aloof from Riggs and his men this was simply a matter of convenience rather than of misanthropy.

On the way out he picked a monographed cream silk shirt from the stack left in the wardrobe by the financier, and slipped into a pair of neatly pressed slacks with a Zurich label. Sealing the double doors behind him—the suite was effectively a glass box inside the outer brick walls—he made his way down the staircase.

He reached the landing stage as Colonel Riggs' cutter, a converted landing craft, pulled in against the catamaran. Riggs stood in the bows, a trim dapper figure, one booted foot up on the ramp, surveying the winding creeks and hanging jungles like an old-time African explorer.

'Good morning, Robert,' he greeted Kerans, jumping down on to the swaying platform of fifty-gallon drums lashed inside a wooden frame. 'Glad you're still here. I've got a job on my hands you can help me with. Can you take the day off from the station?'

Kerans helped him on to the concrete balcony that had once jutted from a seventh-floor suite. 'Of course, Colonel. As a matter of fact, I have already.'

Technically Riggs had overall authority for the testing station and Kerans should have asked his permission, but the relationship between the two men was without ceremony. They had worked together for over three years, as the testing station and its military escort moved slowly northward through the European lagoons, and Riggs was content to let Kerans and Bodkin get on with their work in their own fashion, sufficiently busy himself with the jobs of mapping the shifting keys and harbours and evacuating the last inhabitants. In the latter task he often needed Kerans' help, for most of the people still living on in the sinking cities were either psychopaths or suffering from malnutrition and radiation sickness.

In addition to running the testing station, Kerans served as the unit's medical officer. Many of the people they came across required immediate hospitalization before being flown out in the helicopter to one of the large tank-landing craft ferrying refugees up to Camp Byrd. Injured military personnel marooned on an office block in a deserted swamp, dying recluses unable to separate their own identities from the cities where they had spent their lives, disheartened freebooters who had stayed behind to dive for loot—all these Riggs good humouredly but firmly helped back to safety, Kerans ready at his elbow to administer an analgesic or tranquilliser. Despite his brisk military front, Kerans found the Colonel intelligent and sympathetic, and with a concealed reserve of droll humour. Sometimes he wondered whether to test this by telling the Colonel about Bodkin's Pelycosaur, but on the whole decided against it.

The sergeant concerned in the hoax, a dour conscientious Scotsman called Macready, had climbed up on to the wire cage that enclosed the deck of the cutter and was carefully sweeping away the heavy fronds and vines strewn across it. None of the three other men tried to help him; under their heavy tans their faces looked pinched and drawn, and they sat inertly in a row against a bulkhead. The continuous heat and the massive daily doses of antibiotics drained all energy from them.

As the sun rose over the lagoon, driving clouds of steam into the great golden pall, Kerans felt the terrible stench of the water-line, the sweet compacted smells of dead vegetation and rotting animal carcases. Huge flies spun by, bouncing off the wire cage of the cutter, and giant bats raced across the heating water towards their eyries in the ruined buildings. Beautiful and serene from his balcony a few minutes earlier, Kerans realized that the lagoon was nothing more than a garbage-filled swamp.

'Let's go up on to the deck,' he suggested to Riggs, lowering his voice so that the others would not hear. 'I'll buy you a drink.'

'Good man. I'm glad to see you've really caught on to the grand manner.' Riggs shouted at Macready: 'Sergeant, I'm going up to see if I can get the Doctor's distillation unit to work.' He winked at Kerans as Macready acknowledged this with a skeptical nod, but the subterfuge was harmless. Most of the men carried hip-flasks, and once they secured the sergeant's grudging approval they would bring them out and settle down placidly until the Colonel returned.

Kerans climbed over the window-sill into the bedroom over-looking the jetty. 'What's your problem, Colonel?'

'It's not *my* problem. If anything, in fact, it's yours.'

They trudged up the staircase, Riggs slapping with his baton at the vines entwined around the rail 'Haven't you got the ele-vator working yet? I always thought this place was overrated.' However, he smiled appreciatively when they stepped into the clear ivory-cool air of the penthouse, and sat down thankfully in one of the gilt-legged Louis XV armchairs. 'Well, this is very gracious. You know, Robert, I think you have a natural talent for beachcombing. I may move in here with you. Any vacancies?'

Kerans shook his head, pressing a tab in the wall and waiting as the cocktail bar disgorged itself from a fake bookcase. 'Try the Hilton. The service is better.'

The reply was jocular, but much as he liked Riggs he pre-ferred to see as little of him as possible. At present they were separated by the intervening lagoons, and the constant clatter of the galley and armoury at the base were safely muffled by the jungle. He had known each of the twenty men in the unit for at least a couple of years, but with the exception of Riggs and Sergeant Macready, and a few terse grunts and questions in the sick-bay, he had spoken to none of them for six months. Even his contacts with Bodkin he kept to a minimum. By mutual consent the two biologists had dispensed with the usual pleasantries and small-talk that had sustained them for the first two years dur-ing their sessions of cataloguing and slide preparation at the laboratory.

This growing isolation and self-containment, exhibited by

the other members of the unit and from which only the buoy-
ant Riggs seemed immune, reminded Kerans of the slackening
metabolism and biological withdrawal of all animal forms about
to undergo a major metamorphosis. Sometimes he wondered
what zone of transit he himself was entering, sure that his own
withdrawal was symptomatic not of a dormant schizophrenia,
but of a careful preparation for a radically new environment,
with its own internal landscape and logic, where old categories
of thought would merely be an encumbrance.

HE HANDED a large Scotch to Riggs, then took his own over to
the desk, self-consciously removed some of the books stacked over
the radio console.

'Ever try listening to that thing?' Riggs asked, playfully intro-
ducing a hint of reproof into his voice.

'Never,' Kerans said. 'Is there any point? We know all the news
for the next three million years.'

'You don't. Really, you should switch it on just now and then.
Hear all sorts of interesting things.' He put his drink down and
sat forward. 'For example, this morning you would have heard
that exactly three days from now we're packing up and leaving
for good.' He nodded when Kerans looked around in surprise.
'Came through last night from Byrd. Apparently the water-level
is still rising; all the work we've done has been a total waste—as
I've always maintained, incidentally. The American and Russian
units are being recalled as well. Temperatures at the Equator are
up to one hundred and eighty degrees now, going up steadily,
and the rain belts are continuous as high as the 20th parallel.
There's more silt too—'

He broke off, watching Kerans speculatively. 'What's the matter? Aren't you relieved to be going?'

'Of course,' Kerans said automatically. He was holding an
empty glass, and walked across the room, intending to put it on
the bar, instead found himself absent-mindedly touching the

clock over the mantelpiece. He seemed to be searching the room for something. 'Three days, you said?'

'What do you want—three million?' Riggs grinned broadly. 'Robert, I think you secretly want to stay behind.'

Kerans reached the bar and filled his glass, collecting himself. He had only managed to survive the monotony and boredom of the previous year by deliberately suspending himself outside the normal world of time and space, and the abrupt return to earth had momentarily disconcerted him. In addition, he knew, there were other motives and responsibilities.

'Don't be absurd,' he replied easily. 'I simply hadn't realised that we might withdraw at such short notice. Naturally I'm glad to be going. Though I admit I have enjoyed being here.' He gestured at the suite around them. 'Perhaps it appeals to my *fin de siècle* temperament. Up at Camp Byrd I'll be living in half a mess-tin. The nearest I'll ever get to this sort of thing will be 'Bouncing with Beethoven' on the local radio show.'

Riggs roared at this display of disgruntled humour, then stood up, buttoning his tunic. 'Robert, you're a strange one.'

Kerans finished his drink abruptly. 'Look, Colonel, I don't think I'll be able to help you this morning after all. Something rather urgent has come up.' He noticed Riggs nodding slowly. 'Oh, I see. That was your problem. *My* problem.'

'Right. I saw her last night, and again this morning after the news came through. You'll have to convince her, Robert. At present she refuses point-blank to go. She doesn't realize that this time is the end, that there'll be no more holding units. She may be able to hang on for another six months, but next March, when the rain belts reach here, we won't even be able to get a helicopter in. Anyway, by then no one will care. I told her that and she just walked away.'

Kerans smiled bleakly, visualizing the familiar swirl of hip and haughty stride. 'Beatrice can be difficult sometimes,' he temporized, hoping that she hadn't offended Riggs. It would probably take more than three days to change her mind and he wanted to be sure that the Colonel would still be waiting. 'She's a complex person, lives on many levels. Until they all synchronise she can behave as if she's insane.'

THEY LEFT the suite, Kerans sealing the air-locks and setting the thermostat alarms so that the air would be a pleasant eighty degrees in two hours' time. They made their way down to the landing-stage, Riggs pausing occasionally to savour the cool gilded air in one of the public drawing-rooms overlooking the lagoon, hissing at the snakes which glided softly among the damp, fungus-covered settees. They stepped into the cutter and Macready slammed the door of the cage behind them.

Five minutes later, the catamaran gliding and swirling behind the cutter, they set off from the hotel across the lagoon. Golden waves glimmered up into the boiling air, and the ring of massive plants around them seemed to dance in the heat gradients like a voodoo jungle.

Riggs peered somberly through the cage. 'Thank God for that signal from Byrd. We should have got out years ago. All this detailed mapping of harbours for use in some hypothetical future is absurd. Even if the solar flares subside it will be ten years before there's any serious attempt to reoccupy these cities. By then most of the bigger buildings will have been smothered under the silt. It'll take a couple of divisions to clear the jungle away from this lagoon alone. Bodkin was telling me this morning that already some of the canopies—of non-lignified plants, mark you—are over two hundred feet high. The whole place is nothing but a confounded zoo.'

He took off his peaked cap and rubbed his forehead, then shouted across the mounting roar of the two outboard diesels: 'If Beatrice stays here much longer she *will* be insane. By the way, that reminds me of another reason why we've got to get out.' He glanced across at the tall lonely figure of Sergeant Macready at the tiller, staring fixedly at the breaking water, and at the pinched haunted faces of the other men. 'Tell me, Doctor, how do you sleep these days?'

Puzzled, Kerans turned to look at the Colonel, wondering whether the question obliquely referred to his relationship with Beatrice Dahl. Riggs watched him with his bright intelligent eyes, baton flexed between his neat hands. 'Very soundly,' he replied carefully. 'Never better. Why do you ask?'

But Riggs merely nodded and began to shout instructions at Macready.

2

THE COMING OF THE IGUANAS

SCREECHING LIKE a dispossessed banshee, a large hammer-nosed bat soared straight out of one of the narrow inlets off the creek and swerved straight towards the cutter. Its sonar confused by the labyrinth of giant webs spun across the inlet by the colonies of wolf spiders, it missed the wire hood above Kerans' head by only a few feet, and then sailed away along the line of submerged office blocks, gliding in and out of the huge sail-like fronds of the fern-trees sprouting from their roofs. Suddenly, as it passed one of the projecting cornices, a motionless stone-headed creature snapped out and plucked the bat from the air. There was a brief piercing squawk and Kerans caught a glimpse of the crushed wings clamped in the lizard's jaws. Then the reptile shrank back invisibly among the foliage.

All the way down the creek, perched in the windows of the office blocks and department stores, the iguanas watched them go past, their hard frozen heads jerking stiffly. They launched themselves into the wake of the cutter, snapping at the insects dislodged from the air-weed and rotting logs, then swam through the windows and clambered up the staircases to their former vantage-points, piled three deep across each other. Without the reptiles, the lagoons and the creeks of office blocks half-submerged in the immense heat would have had a strange dream-like beauty, but the iguanas and basilisks brought the fantasy down to earth. As their seats in the one-time boardrooms indicated, the reptiles had taken over the city. Once again they were the dominant form of life.

Looking up at the ancient impassive faces, Kerans could understand the curious fear they roused, re-kindling archaic memories of the terrifying jungles of the Paleocene, when the reptiles had gone down before the emergent mammals, and sense the implacable hatred one zoological class feels towards another that usurps it.

AT THE END of the creek they entered the next lagoon, a wide circle of dark green water almost half a mile in diameter. A lane of red plastic buoys marked a channel towards an opening on the far side. The cutter had a draught of little more than a foot, and as they moved along through the flat water, the sun slanting down behind them opening up the submerged depths, they could see the clear outlines of five- and six-storey buildings looming like giant ghosts, here and there a moss-covered roof breaking the surface as the swell rolled past it.

Sixty feet below the cutter a straight grey promenade stretched away between the buildings, the remains of some former thoroughfare, the rusting humped shells of cars still standing by the kerb. Many of the lagoons in the centre of the city were surrounded by an intact ring of buildings, and consequently little silt had entered them. Free of vegetation, apart from a few drifting clumps of Sargasso weed, the streets and shops had been preserved almost intact, like a reflection in a lake that has somehow lost its original.

The bulk of the city had long since vanished, and only the steel-supported buildings of the central commercial and financial areas had survived the encroaching flood waters. The brick houses and single-storey factories of the suburbs had disappeared completely below the drifting tides of silt. Where these broke surface giant forests reared up into the burning dull-green sky, smothering the former wheatfields of temperate Europe and North America. Impenetrable Mato Grossos sometimes three hundred feet high, they were a nightmare world of competing organic forms returning rapidly to their Paleozoic past, and the only avenues of transit for the United Nations military units were through the lagoon systems that had superimposed themselves on the former cities. But even these were now being clogged with silt and then submerged.

Kerans could remember the unending succession of green twilights that had settled behind them as he and Riggs moved slowly northward across Europe, leaving one city after another, the miasmic vegetation swamping the narrow canals and crowding from roof-top to roof-top.

Now they were to abandon yet another city. Despite the massive construction of the main commercial buildings, it consisted of little more than three principal lagoons, surrounded by a nexus of small lakes fifty yards in diameter and a network of narrow creeks and inlets which wound off, roughly following the original street-plan of the city, into the outlying jungle. Here and there they vanished altogether or expanded into the steaming sheets of open water that were the residues of the former oceans. In turn these gave way to the archipelagoes that coalesced to form the solid jungles of the southern massif.

The military base set up by Riggs and his platoon, which harboured the biological testing station, was in the most southerly of the three lagoons, sheltered by a number of the tallest buildings of the city, thirty-storey blocks in what had once been the downtown financial sector.

As they crossed the lagoon the yellow-striped drum of the floating base was on its sun-ward side, almost obscured in the reflected light, the rotating blades of the helicopter on its roof throwing brilliant lances across the water at them. Two hundred yards down shore was the smaller white-painted hull of the biological testing station, moored against a broad hump-backed building which had formerly been a concert hall.

Kerans gazed up at the rectangular cliffs, enough of the windows intact to remind him of the illustrations of sun-dazzled promenades at Nice, Rio and Miami he had read about as a child in the encyclopedias at Camp Byrd. Curiously, though, despite the potent magic of the lagoon worlds and the drowned cities, he had never felt any interest in their contents, and never bothered to identify in which of the cities he was stationed.

Dr. Bodkin, twenty-five years his senior, had actually lived in several of them, both in Europe and America, and spent most of his spare time punting around the remoter water-ways, searching out former libraries and museums. Not that they contained anything other than his memories.

PERHAPS IT WAS this absence of personal memories that made Kerans indifferent to the spectacle of these sinking civilizations. He had been born and brought up entirely within what had once been known as the Arctic Circle—now a sub-tropical zone with an annual mean temperature of eighty-five degrees—and had come southward only on joining one of the ecological surveys in his early 30's. The vast swamps and jungles had been a fabulous laboratory, the submerged cities little more than elaborate pedestals.

Apart from a few older men such as Bodkin there was no-one who remembered living in them—and even during Bodkin's childhood the cities had been beleaguered citadels, hemmed in by enormous dykes and disintegrated by panic and despair, reluctant Venices to their marriage with the sea. Their charm and beauty lay precisely in their emptiness, in the strange junction of two extremes of nature, like a discarded crown overgrown by wild orchids.

THE SUCCESSION of gigantic geophysical upheavals which had transformed the Earth's climate had made their first impact

some sixty or seventy years earlier. A series of violent and pro-
longed solar storms lasting several years caused by a sudden
instability in the Sun had enlarged the Van Allen belts and
diminished the Earth's gravitational hold upon the outer layers
of the ionosphere. As these vanished into space, depleting the
Earth's barrier against the full impact of solar radiation, temperatures began to climb steadily, the heated atmosphere expanding
outwards into the ionosphere where the cycle was completed.

All over the world, mean temperatures rose by a few degrees
each year. The majority of tropical areas rapidly became unin-
habitable, entire populations migrating north or south from
temperatures of a hundred and thirty and a hundred and forty
degrees. Once-temperate areas became tropical, Europe and
North America sweltering under continuous heat waves, temperatures rarely falling below a hundred degrees. Under the
direction of the United Nations, the colonisation began of the
Antarctic plateau and of the northern borders of the Canadian
and Russian continents.

OVER THIS INITIAL PERIOD of twenty years a gradual adjust-
ment of life took place to meet the altered climate. A slackening of the previous tempo was inevitable, and there was little
spare energy available to cut back the encroaching jungles of the
equatorial region. Not only was the growth of all plant forms
accelerated, but the higher levels of radio-activity increased the
rate at which mutations occurred. The first freak botanical forms
appeared, recalling the giant tree-ferns of the Carboniferous
period, and there was a drastic upsurge of all lower plant and
animal forms.

The arrival of these distant forbears was overlayed by the second major geophysical upheaval. The continued heating of the
atmosphere had begun to melt the polar ice-caps. The entrained
ice-seas of the Antarctic plateau broke and dissolved, tens of
thousands of glaciers around the Arctic Circle, from Greenland
and Northern Europe, Russia and North America, poured them-

selves into the sea, millions of acres of permafrost liquefied into gigantic rivers.

Here again the rise of global water-levels would have been little more than a few feet, but the huge discharging channels carried with them billions of tons of top-soil. Massive deltas formed at their mouths, extending the continental coastlines and damming up the oceans. Their effective spread shrank from two-thirds of the world's area to only slightly more than half.

Driving the submerged silt before them, the new seas completely altered the shape and contours of the continents. The Mediterranean contracted into a system of inland lakes, the British Isles was linked again with northern France. The Middle West of the United States, filled by the Mississippi as it drained the Rocky Mountains, became an enormous gulf opening into the Hudson Bay, while the Caribbean Sea was transformed into a desert of silt and salt flats. Europe became a system of giant lagoons, centred on the principal low-lying cities, inundated by the silt carried southwards by the expanding rivers.

DURING THE NEXT thirty years the pole-ward migration of populations continued. A few fortified cities defied the rising water-levels and the encroaching jungles, building elaborate sea-walls around their perimeters, but one by one these were breached. Only within the former Arctic and Antarctic Circles was life tolerable. The oblique incidence of the sun's rays provided a shield against the more powerful radiation. Cities on higher ground in mountainous areas nearer the Equator had been abandoned, despite their cooler temperatures, because of the diminished atmospheric protection.

It was this last factor which provided its own solution to the problem of re-settling the migrant populations of the new Earth. The steady decline in mammalian fertility, and the growing ascendancy of amphibian and reptile forms best adapted to an aquatic life in the lagoons and swamps, inverted the ecological balances, and by the time of Kerans' birth at Camp Byrd, a city of ten thousand in Northern Greenland, it was estimated that fewer than five million people were still living on the polar caps.

The birth of a child had become a comparative rarity, and only one marriage in ten yielded any offspring. As Kerans sometimes reminded himself, the genealogical tree of mankind was systematically pruning itself, apparently moving backwards in time, and a point might ultimately be reached where a second Adam and Eve found themselves alone in a new Eden.

RIGG NOTICED HIM smiling to himself at this conceit. 'What's amusing you, Robert? Another of your obscure jokes? Don't try to explain it to me.'

'I was just casting myself in a new role.' Kerans looked out over the ramp at the office blocks sliding past twenty feet away, the wash from the cutter splashing through the open windows along the water-line. The sharp tang of wet lime contrasted freshly with the over-sweet odours of the vegetation. Macready had taken them into the shadow of the buildings and it was pleasantly cool behind the breaking spray.

Across the lagoon he could see the portly bare-chested figure of Dr. Bodkin on the starboard bridge of the testing station, the Paisley cummerbund around his waist and the green celluloid shade shielding his eyes making him look like a riverboat gambler on his morning off. He was plucking the orange-sized berries from the ferns overhanging the station and tossing them up at the chittering marmosets dangling from the branches above his head, egging them on with playful shouts and whistles. Fifty feet away, on a projecting cornice, a trio of iguanas watched with stony disapproval, whipping their tails slowly from side to side in a gesture of impatience.

Macready swung the tiller, and they pivoted in a fan of spray into the lee of a tall white-faced building which lifted a full

twenty storeys out of the water. The roof of an adjacent smaller
block served as a jetty, next to which was moored a rusty white-
hulled power cruiser. The raked perspex windows of the driving
cabin were cracked and stained, and the exhaust vents leaked a
scaly oil on to the water.

AS THE CUTTER jockeyed in behind the power cruiser under
Macready's expert hand, they clambered over to the wire door,
jumped down on to the jetty and crossed a narrow metal gangway that led into the apartment block. The walls of the corridor
were slick with moisture, huge patches of mould feeding on the
plaster, but the elevator was still working, powered by an emer-
gency diesel. They rose slowly towards the roof, and stepped out
on to the upper level of the duplex, then walked down a service
corridor to the outer deck.

DIRECTLY BELOW THEM was the lower level, a small swimming pool with a covered patio, bright deck-chairs drawn up in
the shade by the diving board. Yellow venetian blinds masked
the windows around three sides of the pool, but through the
vanes they could see the cool shadows in the interior lounge,
the glint of cut-glass and silver on the occasional tables. In the
dim light under the striped blue awning at the rear of the patio
was a long chromium counter, as inviting as an air-conditioned
bar seen from a dusty street, glasses and decanters reflected in a
diamond-paned mirror. Everything in this private haven seemed
clean and discreet, thousands of miles away from the fly-blown
vegetation and tepid jungle water twenty storeys below.

Beyond the far end of the pool, screened by an ornamental
balcony, was a wide, open view of the lagoon, the city emerging
from the encroaching jungle, flat sheets of silver water expanding towards the green blur along the southern horizon. Massive
silt banks lifted their backs through the surface, a light yellow
fur along their spines marking the emergence of the first giant
bamboo groves.

The helicopter rose from its platform on the roof of the base and arced upwards into the air towards them, the pilot swinging the tail as he changed direction, then roared overhead, two men in the open hatchway searching the rooftops with binoculars.

Beatrice Dahl lay back on one of the deck-chairs, her long oiled body gleaming in the shadows like a sleeping python. The pink-tipped fingers of one hand rested lightly on an ice-filled glass on a table beside her, while the other hand turned slowly through the pages of a magazine. Wide blue-black sunglasses hid her smooth sleek face, but Kerans noted the slightly sullen pout of her firm lower lip. Presumably Riggs had annoyed her, forcing her to accept the logic of his argument.

The Colonel paused at the rail, looking down at the beautiful supple body with ungrudging approval. Noticing him, Beatrice pulled off her sunglasses, then tightened the loose back-straps of her bikini under her arms. Her eyes glinted quietly.

'All right, you two, get on with it. I'm not a strip show.'

Riggs chuckled and trotted down the white metal stairway, Kerans at his heels, wondering how he was going to persuade Beatrice to leave her private sanctuary.

'My dear Miss Dahl, you should be flattered that I keep coming to see you,' Riggs told her, lifting back the awning and sitting down on one of the chairs. 'Besides, as the military governor of this area'—here he winked playfully at Kerans—'I have certain responsibilities towards you. And vice versa.'

Beatrice regarded him briefly with a jaundiced eye and reached out to turn up the volume of the radiogram behind her. 'Oh God . . .' She muttered some further, less polite imprecation under her breath and looked up at Kerans. 'And what about you, Robert? What brings you out so early in the day?'

Kerans shrugged, smiling at her amiably. 'I missed you.'

'Good boy. I thought perhaps that the *gauleiter* here had been trying to frighten you with his horror stories.'

'Well, he has, as a matter of fact.' Kerans took the magazine propped against Beatrice's knee and leafed through it idly. It was a forty-year-old issue of Paris *Vogue*, from its icy pages evidently kept somewhere in cold storage. He dropped it on the green-tiled floor. 'Bea, it looks as if we'll all have to leave here in a couple of days' time. The Colonel and his men are pulling out for good. We can't very well stay on after he's gone.'

'We?' she repeated dryly. 'I didn't know there was any chance of your staying behind?'

Kerans glanced involuntarily at Riggs, who was watching him steadily. 'There isn't,' he said firmly. 'You know what I mean. There'll be a lot to do in the next forty-eight hours. Try not to complicate things by making a last emotional stand.'

Before the girl could cut back at Kerans, Riggs added smoothly: 'The temperature is still going up, Miss Dahl, you won't find it easy to stand one hundred and thirty degrees when the fuel for your generator runs out. The big Equatorial rain belts are moving northward, and they'll be here in a couple of months. When they leave, and the cloud cover goes, the water in that pool—' he indicated the tank of steaming, insect-strewn fluid—'will damn' nearly boil. What with the Type X Anopheles, skin cancers and the iguanas shrieking all night down below, you'll get precious little sleep.' Closing his eyes, he added pensively: 'That is, assuming that you still want any.'

At this last remark the girl's mouth fretted slightly. Kerans realized that the quiet ambiguity in Riggs' voice when he asked how the biologist slept had not been directed at his relationship with Beatrice.

The Colonel went on: 'In addition, some of the human scavengers driven northward out of the Mediterranean lagoons won't be too easy to deal with.'

Beatrice tossed her long black hair over one shoulder. 'I'll keep the door locked, Colonel.'

Irritated, Kerans snapped: 'For God's sake, Beatrice, what are you trying to prove? These self-destructive impulses may be amusing to play with now, but when we've gone they won't be so funny. The Colonel's only trying to help you——he doesn't really give a hoot whether you stay behind or not.'

Riggs let out a brief laugh. 'Well, I wouldn't say that. But if the thought of my personal concern worries you so much you can just put it down to duty.'

'That's interesting, Colonel. I've always understood that our duty was to stay on here as long as possible and make every sacrifice necessary to that end. Or at least'——here the familiar gleam of sharp humour crossed her eyes——'that was the reason my grandfather was given when the Government confiscated most of his property.' She noticed Riggs peering over his shoulder at the bar. 'What's the matter, Colonel? Looking for your punka-wallah? I'm not going to get you a drink, if that's what you're after. I think you men only come up here to booze.'

Riggs stood up. 'All right, Miss Dahl. I give in. I'll see you later, Doctor.' He saluted Beatrice with a smile. 'Some time tomorrow I'll send the cutter over to collect your gear, Miss Dahl.'

WHEN RIGGS HAD GONE Kerans lay back in his chair, watching the helicopter circle over the adjacent lagoon. Now and then it dived along the water's edge, the down-draught from its rotor blades beating through the flapping fronds of the fern-trees, driving the iguanas across the rooftops. Beatrice brought a drink from the bar and sat down on the chair at his feet.

'I wish you wouldn't analyse me in front of that man, Robert.' She handed him the drink and then leaned against his knees, resting her chin on one wrist. Usually she looked sleek and well-fed, but her expression today seemed tired and wistful.

'I'm sorry,' Kerans apologised. 'Perhaps I was really analysing myself. Riggs' ultimatum came as a bit of a surprise; I wasn't expecting to leave so soon.'

'You are going to leave, then?'

Kerans paused. The automatic player in the radiogram switched from Beethoven's Pastoral to the Seventh, Toscanini giving way to Bruno Walter. All day, without a break, it played through the cycle of nine symphonies. He searched for an answer, the change of mood, to the somber opening motif of the Seventh, overlaying his indecision.

'I suppose I want to, but I haven't yet found an adequate reason. Satisfying one's emotional needs isn't enough. There's got to be a more valid motive. Perhaps these sunken lagoons simply remind me of the drowned world of my uterine childhood—if so, the best thing is to leave straight away. Everything Riggs says is true. There's little hope of standing up to the rainstorms and the malaria.'

He placed his hand on her forehead, feeling her temperature like a child's. 'What did Riggs mean when he said you wouldn't sleep well? That was the second time this morning he mentioned it.'

Beatrice looked away for a moment. 'Oh, nothing. I've just had one or two peculiar nightmares recently. A lot of people get them. Forget it. Tell me, Robert, seriously—if I decide to stay on here, would you? You could share this apartment.'

Kerans grinned. 'Trying to tempt me, Bea? What a question. Remember, not only are you the most beautiful woman here, but you're the only woman. Nothing is more essential than a basis for comparison. Adam had no aesthetic sense, or he would have realized that Eve was a pretty haphazard piece of work.'

'You are being frank today.' Beatrice stood up and went over to the edge of the pool. She swept her hair back off her forehead with both hands, her long supple body gleaming against the sunlight. 'But is there as much urgency as Riggs claims? We've got the cruiser.'

'It's a wreck. The first serious storm will split it open like a rusty can.'

Nearing noon, the heat on the terrace had become uncomfortable and they left the patio and went indoors. Double venetian blinds filtered a thin sunlight into the low wide lounge, and the refrigerated air was cool and soothing. Beatrice stretched out on a long pale-blue elephant hide sofa, one hand playing with the fleecy pile of the carpet. The apartment had been one of her grandfather's *pieds à terre*, and Beatrice's home since her parents' death shortly after her birth. She had been brought up under the supervision of the grandfather, who had been a lonely, eccentric tycoon (the sources of his wealth Kerans had never established: when he asked Beatrice, shortly after he and Riggs stumbled upon her penthouse eyrie, she replied succinctly: 'Let's say he was in money') and a great patron of the arts in his earlier days. His tastes leaned particularly towards the experimental and bizarre, and Kerans often wondered how far his personality and its strange internal perspectives had been carried forward into his grand-daughter. Over the mantelpiece was a huge painting by the early 20th-century Surrealist, Delvaux, in which ashen-faced women danced naked to the waist with dandified skeletons in tuxedos against a spectral bone-like landscape. On another wall one of Max Ernst's self-devouring phantasmagoric jungles screamed silently to itself, like the sump of some insane unconscious.

For a few moments Kerans stared quietly at the dim yellow annulus of Ernst's sun glowering through the exotic vegetation, a curious feeling of memory and recognition signaling through his brain. Far more potent than the Beethoven, the image of the archaic sun burned against his mind, illuminating the fleeting shadows that darted fitfully through its profoundest deeps.

'Beatrice.'

She looked up at him as he walked across to her, a light frown crossing her eyes. 'What's the matter, Robert?'

Kerans hesitated, suddenly aware that, however brief and imperceptible, a moment of significant time had elapsed, car-rying him forward with its passage into a zone of commitment from which he would not be able to withdraw.

'You realise that if we let Riggs go without us we don't merely leave here later. We *stay*.'

3

TOWARDS A NEW PSYCHOLOGY

BERTHING THE CATAMARAN against the landing stage, Kerans shipped the outboard and then made his way up the gangway into the base. As he let himself through the screen hatch he looked back over his shoulder across the lagoon, and caught a brief glimpse through the heat waves of Beatrice standing at her balcony rail. When he waved, however, she characteristically turned away without responding.

'One of her moody days, Doctor?' Sergeant Macready stepped from the guard cubicle, a trace of humour relaxing his beak-like face. 'She's a strange one, all right.'

Kerans shrugged. 'These tough bachelor girls, you know, Sergeant. If you're not careful they frighten the wits out of you. I've been trying to persuade her to pack up and come with us. With a little luck I think she will.'

Macready peered shrewdly at the distant roof of the apartment house. 'I'm glad to hear you say so, Doctor,' he ventured noncommittally, but Kerans was unable to decide if his scepticism was directed at Beatrice or himself.

Whether or not they finally stayed behind, Kerans had resolved to maintain the pretence that they were leaving—every spare minute of the next three days would be needed to consolidate their supplies and steal whatever extra equipment they required from the base stores. Kerans had still not made up his mind—once away from Beatrice his indecision returned (ruefully he wondered if she was deliberately trying to confuse him, Pandora with her killing mouth and witch's box of desires and frustrations, unpredictably opening and shutting the lid)— but rather than stumble about in a state of tortured uncertainty, which Riggs and Bodkin would soon diagnose, he decided to postpone a final reckoning until the last moment possible. Much as he loathed the base, he knew that the sight of it actually sailing off would act as a wonderful catalyst for emotions of fear and panic, and any more abstract motives for staying behind would soon be abandoned. A year earlier, he had been accidentally marooned on a small key while taking an unscheduled geomagnetic reading, the departure siren muffled by his headphones as he crouched over his instruments in an old basement bunker. When he emerged ten minutes later and found the base six hundred yards away across a widening interval of flat water he had felt like a child parted forever from its mother, barely managed to control his panic in time to fire a warning shell from his flare pistol.

'Dr. Bodkin asked me to call you as soon as you arrived, sir. Lieutenant Hardman hasn't been too happy this morning.'

Kerans nodded, glancing up and down the empty deck. He had taken lunch with Beatrice, knowing that the base was deserted in the afternoons. Half the crew were away with either Riggs or the helicopter, the rest asleep in their bunks, and he had hoped to carry out a private tour of the stores and armoury. Now unluckily, Macready, the Colonel's ever-alert watch-dog, was hanging about at his heels, ready to escort him up the companion-way to the sick-bay on B-Deck.

Kerans studiously examined a pair of Anopheles mosquitoes which had slipped through the wire hatch behind him. 'They're still getting in,' he pointed out to Macready.

'What's happened to the double screening you were supposed to be putting up?'

Swatting at the mosquitoes with his forage cap, Macready looked around uncertainly. A secondary layer of screening around the wire mesh enclosing the base had long been one of Colonel Riggs' pet projects. At times he would tell Macready to detail a squad to carry out the work, but as this involved sitting on a wooden trestle in the open sunlight in the centre of a cloud of mosquitoes only a few token sections around Riggs' cabin had been completed. Now that they were moving northward the utility of the project had faded, but Macready's Presbyterian conscience, once roused, refused to let him rest.

'I'll get the men on to it this evening, Doctor,' he assured Kerans, pulling a ball-pen and note—book from his hip pocket.

'No hurry, Sergeant, but if you've nothing better to do. I know the Colonel's very keen.' Kerans left him squinting along the metal louvres and walked off down the deck. As soon as he was out of sight he stepped through the first doorway.

C-Deck, the lowest of the three decks comprising the base, contained the crew's quarters and galley. Two or three men lay about among their tropical gear in the cabins, but the recreation-room was empty, a radio playing to itself by the table-tennis tournament board in the corner. Kerans paused, listening to the strident rhythms of the guitar music, overlayed by the distant blare of the helicopter circling over the next lagoon, then made his way down the central stair—well which led to the armoury and workshops housed in the pontoon.

Three-quarters of the hull was occupied by the 2,000-h.p. diesels which powered the twin screws, and by the oil and aviation fuel tanks, and the workshops had been temporarily transferred during the final aerial sweeps to two vacant offices on A-Deck, beside the officers' quarters, so that the mechanics could service the helicopter with the maximum speed.

The armoury was closed when Kerans entered, a single light

burning in the technical corporal's glass-walled booth. Kerans gazed around the heavy wooden benches and cabinets lined with carbines and submachine-guns. Steel rods through the trigger guards locked the weapons into their cases, and he idly touched the heavy stocks, doubting whether he could handle any of the weapons even if he stole one. In a drawer at the testing station was a Colt .45 and fifty rounds issued to him three years earlier. Once a year he made an official return on the ammunition discharged—in his case none—and exchanged the unused shells for a fresh issue, but he had never tried to fire the pistol.

On his way out he scanned the dark green ammunition boxes stacked around the wall below the cabinets, all of them double-padlocked. He was passing the booth when the light through the door illuminated the dusty labels on a row of metal cartons below one of the work benches.

'Hy-Dyne.' On an impulse Kerans stopped, pushed his fingers through the wire cage and brushed the dust off a label, tracing the formula with his fingers. 'Cyclotrimethylene-trinitramine: Gas discharge speed—8,000 metres/second.'

Speculating on the possible uses of the explosive—it would be a brilliant *tour de force* to sink one of the office buildings into the exit creek after Riggs had left, blocking any attempt to return— he leaned his elbows on the bench, playing absent-mindedly with a 4-inch-diameter brass compass that had been left for repair. The calibrated annulus was loose and had been rotated a full 180 degrees, the point emphasised with a chalked cross.

Still thinking about the explosive, and the possibility of stealing detonators and fuse-wire, Kerans rubbed away the blunt chalk marks and then lifted the compass and weighed it in his hand. Leaving the armoury, he began to climb the stairway, uncaging the compass and letting the pointer dance and float. A sailor walked past along C-Deck, and Kerans quickly slipped the compass into his jacket pocket.

Suddenly, as he visualised himself throwing his weight on to the handles of a plunger box and catapulting Riggs, the base and the testing station into the next lagoon, he stopped and steadied himself against the rail. Smiling ruefully at the absurdity of the fantasy, he wondered why he had indulged it.

Then he noticed the heavy cylinder of the compass dragging at his jacket. For a moment he peered down at it thoughtfully.

'Look out, Kerans,' he murmured to himself. 'You're living on two levels.'

FIVE MINUTES LATER, when he entered the sick-bay on B-Deck, he found more urgent problems facing him.

Three men were being treated for heat ulcers in the dispensary, but the main twelve-bed ward was empty. Kerans nodded to the corporal issuing penicillin band-aids and walked through to the small single ward on the starboard side of the deck.

The door was closed, but as he turned the handle he could hear the restless heaving motion of the cot, followed by a fractious muttering from the patient and Dr. Bodkin's equable but firm reply. For a few moments the latter continued to speak in a low even monologue, punctuated by a few shrugging protests and concluded by an interval of tired silence.

Lieutenant Hardman, the senior pilot of the helicopter (now being flown by his co-pilot, Sergeant Daley) was the only other commissioned member of the survey unit, and until the last three months had served as Riggs' deputy and chief executive officer. A burly, intelligent but somewhat phlegmatic man of about 30, he had quietly kept himself apart from the other members of the unit. Something of an amateur naturalist, he made his own descriptive notes of the changing flora and fauna, employing a taxonomic system of his own devising. In one of his few unguarded moments he had shown the notebooks to Kerans, then abruptly withdrawn into himself when Kerans tactfully pointed out that the classifications were confused.

For the first two years Hardman had been the perfect buffer

between Riggs and Kerans. The rest of the crew took their cue from the Lieutenant, and this had the advantage, from Kerans' point of view, that the group never developed that sense of happy cohesion a more extravert second-in-command might have instilled, and which would have soon made life unbearable. The loose fragmentary relationships aboard the base, where a replacement was accepted as a fully paid up member of the crew within five minutes and no one cared whether he had been there two days or two years, was largely a reflection of Hardman's temperament. When he organised a basket-ball match or a regatta out on the lagoon there was no self-conscious boisterousness, but a laconic indifference to whether anyone took part or not.

Recently, however, the more sombre elements in Hardman's personality had begun to predominate. Two months earlier he complained to Kerans of intermittent insomnia—often, from Beatrice Dahl's apartment, Kerans would watch him long after midnight standing in the moonlight beside the helicopter on the roof of the base, looking out across the silent lagoon—and then took advantage of an attack of malaria to excuse himself from flying duty. Confined to his cabin for up to a week on end, he steadily retreated into his private world, going through his old notebooks and running his fingers, like a blind man reading Braille, across the glass display cases with their few mounted butterflies and giant moths.

The malaise had not been difficult to diagnose. Kerans recognised the same symptoms he had seen in himself, an accelerated entry into his own 'zone of transit', and left the Lieutenant alone, asking Bodkin to call in periodically.

Curiously, however, Bodkin had taken a more serious view of Hardman's illness.

PUSHING BACK the door, Kerans stepped quietly into the darkened room, pausing in the corner by the ventilator shaft as Bodkin raised a monitory hand towards him. The blinds over the

windows were drawn, and to Kerans' surprise the air-conditioning unit had been switched off. The air pumped in through
the ventilator was never more than twenty degrees below the
ambient temperatures of the lagoon, and the air-conditioner normally kept the room at an even 70 degrees. Bodkin had not only
switched this off but plugged a small electric fire into the shaver
socket over the hand-basin mirror. Kerans remembered him
building the fire in the laboratory at the testing station, fitting a
dented paraboloid mirror around the single filament. Little more
than a couple of watts in strength, the fire seemed to emit an
immense heat, blazing out into the small room like a furnace
mouth, and within a few seconds Kerans felt the sweat gathering
around his neck. Bodkin, sitting on the metal bedside chair with
his back to the fire, was still wearing his white cotton jacket,
stained by two wide patches of sweat that touched between his
shoulder blades, and in the dim red light Kerans could see the
moisture beading off his head like drops of white-hot lead.

Hardman lay slumped back on one elbow, his broad chest
and shoulders filling the backrest, big hands holding the leads
of a pair of headphones clasped to his ears. His narrow, large-
jawed face was pointed towards Kerans, but his eyes were fixed
on the electric fire. Projected by the parabolic bowl, a circular
disc of intense red light three feet in diameter covered the wall
of the cabin, Hardman's head at its centre, like an enormous
glowing halo.

A faint scratching noise came from a portable record-player
on the floor at Bodkin's feet, a single three-inch disc spinning on
its turntable. Generated mechanically by the pick-up head, the
almost imperceptible sounds of a deep slow drumming reached
Kerans, lost as the record ended and Bodkin switched off the
player. Quickly he jotted something down on a desk-pad, then
turned off the electric fire and put on the bedside lamp.

Shaking his head slowly, Hardman pulled off the headphones
and handed them to Bodkin.

'This is a waste of time, Doctor. These records are insane; you can put any interpretation you like on them.' He settled his heavy limbs uncomfortably in the narrow cot. Despite the heat, there was little sweat on his face and bare chest, and he watched the fading embers of the electric fire as if reluctant to see them vanish.

Bodkin stood up and put the record-player on his chair, wrapping the headphones around the case. 'Perhaps that's the point, Lieutenant—a sort of aural Rorschach. I think the last record was the most evocative, don't you agree?'

Hardman shrugged with studied vagueness, evidently reluctant to co-operate with Bodkin and concede even the smallest point. But despite this Kerans felt that he had been glad to take part in the experiment, using it for his own purposes.

'Maybe,' Hardman said grudgingly. 'But I'm afraid it didn't suggest a concrete image.'

Bodkin smiled, aware of Hardman's resistance but prepared for the moment to give in to him. 'Don't apologise, Lieutenant; believe me, that was our most valuable session so far.' He waved to Kerans. 'Come in, Robert, I'm sorry it's so warm—Lieutenant Hardman and I have been conducting a small experiment together. I'll tell you about it when we go back to the station. Now'—he pointed to a contraption on the bedside table which appeared to be two alarm clocks clipped back to back, crude metal extensions from the hands interlocking like the legs of two grappling spiders—'keep this thing running as long as you can, it shouldn't be too difficult, all you have to do is re-set both alarms after each twelve-hour cycle. They'll wake you once every ten minutes, just enough time for you to get sufficient rest before you slide off the pre-conscious shelf into deep sleep. With luck there'll be no more dreams.'

Hardman smiled sceptically, glancing up briefly at Kerans. 'I think you're being over-optimistic, Doctor. What you really mean is that I won't be *aware* of them.' He picked up a well-thumbed green file, his botanical diary, and began to turn the pages mechanically. 'Sometimes I think I have the dreams continuously, every minute of the day. Perhaps we all do.'

His tone was relaxed and unhurried, despite the fatigue which had drained the skin around his eyes and mouth, making his long jaw seem even more lantern-like. Kerans realised that the malaise, whatever its source, had barely touched the central core of the man's ego. The element of tough self-sufficiency in Hardman was as strong as ever, if anything stronger, like a steel blade springing against a fencing post and revealing its sinews.

Bodkin dabbed at his face with a yellow silk handkerchief, watching Hardman thoughtfully. His grimy cotton jacket and haphazard attire, coupled with his puffy, quinine-tinted skin, misleadingly made him look like a seedy quack, masking a sharp and unresting intelligence. 'Perhaps you're right, Lieutenant. In fact, some people used to maintain that consciousness is nothing more than a special category of the cytoplasmic coma, that the capacities of the central nervous system are as fully developed and extended by the dream life as they are during what we call the waking state. But we have to adopt an empirical approach, try whatever remedy we can. Don't you agree, Kerans?'

Kerans nodded. The temperature in the cabin had begun to fall, and he felt himself breathing more freely. 'A change of climate will probably help as well.' There was a dull clatter outside as one of the metal scows being hauled up in its davits clanged against the hull. He added: 'The atmosphere in these lagoons is pretty enervating. Three days from now when we leave I think we'll all show a marked improvement.'

He assumed that Hardman had been told of their imminent departure, but the Lieutenant looked up at him sharply, lowering his notebook. Bodkin began to clear his throat and abruptly started talking about the danger of draughts from the ventilator. For a few seconds Kerans and Hardman watched each other steadily, and then the Lieutenant nodded briefly to himself and resumed his reading, carefully noting the time from the bed-side clocks.

Angry with himself, Kerans went over to the window, his back turned to the others. He realised that he had told Hardman deliberately, unconsciously hoping to elicit precisely this response, and knowing full well why Bodkin had withheld the news. Without the shadow of a doubt he had warned Hardman, telling him that whatever tasks he had to carry out, whatever internal perspectives to bring to a common focus, this should be completed within three days.

Kerans looked down irritably at the alarm device on the table, resenting his diminishing control over his own motives. First the meaningless theft of the compass, and now this act of gratuitous sabotage. However varied his faults, in the past he had always believed them to be redressed by one outstanding virtue—a com-plete and objective awareness of the motives behind his actions. If he was sometimes prone to undue delays this was a result, not of irresolution, but of a reluctance to act at all where complete self-awareness was impossible—his affair with Beatrice Dahl, tilted by so many conflicting passions, from day to day walked a narrow tightrope of a thousand restraints and cautions.

In a belated attempt to reassert himself, he said to Hard-man: 'Don't forget the clock, Lieutenant. If I were you, I'd set the alarm so that it rings continuously.'

LEAVING THE SICK-BAY, they made their way down to the jetty and climbed into Kerans' catamaran. Too tired to start the motor, Kerans slowly pulled them along the overhead hawser stretched between the base and the testing station. Bodkin sat in the bows, the record player held between his knees like a brief-case, blinking in the bright sunlight that spangled the broken surface of the sluggish green water. His plump face, topped by an untidy grey thatch, seemed preoccupied and wistful, scanning the surrounding ring of half-submerged buildings like a weary ship's chandler being rowed around a harbour for the thousandth time. As they neared the testing station the helicopter roared in overhead and alighted, its impact tilting the base and dipping the hawser into the water, then tautening it and cascading a brief shower across their shoulders. Bodkin cursed under his breath, but they were dry within a few seconds. Although it was well after four o'clock, the sun filled the sky, turning it into an enormous blow-torch and forcing them to lower their eyes to the water-line. Now and then, in the glass curtain-walling of the surrounding buildings, they would see countless reflections of the sun move across the surface in huge sheets of fire, like the blazing facetted eyes of gigantic insects.

A TWO-STOREY DRUM some fifty feet in diameter, the testing station had a dead weight of twenty tons. The lower deck contained the laboratory, the upper the two biologists' quarters and the chartroom and offices. A small bridge traversed the roof, and housed the temperature and humidity registers, rainfall gauge and radiation counters. Clumps of dried air-weed and red kelp were encrusted across the bitumened plates of the pontoon, shrivelled and burnt by the sun before they could reach the railing around the laboratory, while a dense refuse-filled mass of sargassum and spirogyra cushioned their impact as they reached the narrow jetty, oozing and subsiding like an immense soggy raft.

They entered the cool darkness of the laboratory and sat down at their desks below the semicircle of fading programme schedules which reached to the ceiling behind the dais, looking down over the clutter of benches and fume cupboards like a dusty mural. The schedules on the left, dating from their first year of work, were packed with detailed entries and minutely labelled arrow sprays, but those on the right thinned out progressively, until a few pencilled scrawls in giant longhand loops sealed off all but one or two of the ecological corridors. Many of the card-

board screens had sprung off their drawing pins, and hung forwards into the air like the peeling hull-plates of a derelict ship,
moored against its terminal pier and covered with gnomic and
meaningless graffiti.

Idly tracing a large compass dial with his finger in the dust on
the desk-top, Kerans waited for Bodkin to provide some explanation for his curious experiments with Hardman. But Bodkin
settled himself comfortably behind the muddle of box-files and
catalogue trays on his desk, then opened the record player and
removed the disc from the table, spinning it reflectively between
his hands.

Kerans began: 'I'm sorry I let slip that we were leaving in three
days' time. I hadn't realized you'd kept that from Hardman.'

Bodkin shrugged, dismissing this as of little importance. 'It's
a complex situation, Robert. Having gone a few steps towards
unravelling it, I didn't want to introduce another slip-knot.'

'But why not tell him?' Kerans pressed, hoping obliquely to
absolve himself of his slight feeling of guilt. 'Surely the prospect
of leaving might well jolt him out of his lethargy?'

Bodkin lowered his glasses to the end of his nose and regarded
Kerans quizzically. 'It doesn't seem to have had that effect on
you, Robert. Unless I'm very much mistaken, you look rather
un-jolted. Why should Hardman's reactions be any different?'

Kerans smiled. 'Touché, Alan. I don't want to interfere, having
more or less dropped Hardman into your lap, but what exactly
are you and he playing about with—why the electric heater and
alarm clocks?'

Bodkin slid the gramophone record into a rack of miniature
discs on the shelf behind him. He looked up at Kerans and for a
few moments watched him with the mild but penetrating gaze
with which he had observed Hardman, and Kerans realised that
their relationship, until now that of colleagues confiding completely in each other, had become closer to that of observer and
subject. After a pause Bodkin glanced away at the programme

charts, and Kerans chuckled involuntarily. To himself he said: Damn the old boy, he's got me up there now with the algae and nautiloids; next he'll be playing his records at me.

Bodkin stood up and pointed to the three rows of laboratory benches, crowded with vivaria and specimen jars, pages from notebooks pinned to the fume hoods above them.

'Tell me, Robert, if you had to sum up the last three years' work in a single conclusion, how would you set about it?'

Kerans hesitated, then gestured off-handedly. 'It wouldn't be too difficult.' He saw that Bodkin expected a serious answer, and composed his thoughts. 'Well, one could simply say that in response to the rises in temperature, humidity and radiation levels the flora and fauna of this planet are beginning to assume once again the forms they displayed the last time such conditions were present—roughly speaking, the Triassic period.'

'Correct.' Bodkin strolled off among the benches. 'During the last three years, Robert, you and I have examined something like five thousand species in the animal kingdom, seen literally tens of thousands of new plant varieties. Everywhere the same pattern has unfolded, countless mutations completely transforming the organisms to adapt them for survival in the new environment. Everywhere there's been the same avalanche backwards into the past—so much so that the few complex organisms which have managed to retain a foothold unchanged on the slope look distinctly anomalous—a handful of amphibians, the birds, and *Man*. It's a curious thing that although we've carefully catalogued the backward journeys of so many plants and animals, we've ignored the most important creature on this planet.'

Kerans laughed. 'I'll willingly take a small bow there, Alan. But what are you suggesting—that *Homo sapiens* is about to transform himself into Cro-Magnon and Java Man, and ultimately into *Sinanthropus?* Unlikely, surely. Wouldn't that merely be Lamarckism in reverse?'

'Agreed. I'm *not* suggesting that.' Bodkin leaned against one of the benches, feeding a handful of peanuts to a small marmoset caged in a converted fume cupboard. 'Though obviously after two or three hundred million years *Homo sapiens* might well die out and our little cousin here become the highest form of life on the planet. However, a biological process isn't completely reversible.' He pulled the silk handkerchief out of his pocket and flicked it at the marmoset, which flinched away tremulously. 'If *we* return to the jungle we'll dress for dinner.'

He went over to a window and gazed out through the mesh screen, the overhang of the deck above shutting out all but a narrow band of the intense sunlight. Steeped in the vast heat, the lagoon lay motionlessly, palls of steam humped over the water like elephantine spectres.

'But I'm really thinking of something else. Is it only the external landscape which is altering? How often recently most of us have had the feeling of déjà vu, of having seen all this before, in fact of remembering these swamps and lagoons all too well. However selective the conscious mind may be, most biological memories are unpleasant ones, echoes of danger and terror. Nothing endures for so long as fear. Everywhere in nature one sees evidence of innate releasing mechanisms literally millions of years old, which have lain dormant through thousands of generations but retained their power undiminished. The field-rat's inherited image of the hawk's silhouette is the classic example—even a paper silhouette drawn across a cage sends it rushing frantically for cover. And how else can you explain the universal but completely groundless loathing of the spider, only one species of which has ever been known to sting? Or the equally surprising—in view of their comparative rarity—hatred of snakes and reptiles? Simply because we all carry within us a submerged memory of the time when the giant spiders were lethal, and when the reptiles were the planet's dominant life form.'

Feeling the brass compass which weighed down his pocket,

Kerans said: 'So you're frightened that the increased temperature and radiation are alerting similar IRM's in our own minds?'

'Not in our minds, Robert. These are the oldest memories on Earth, the time-codes carried in every chromosome and gene. Every step we've taken in our evolution is a milestone inscribed with organic memories—from the enzymes controlling the carbon dioxide cycle to the organization of the brachial plexus and the nerve pathways of the Pyramid cells in the mid-brain, each is a record of a thousand decisions taken in the face of a sudden physico-chemical crisis. Just as psychoanalysis reconstructs the original traumatic situation in order to release the repressed material, so we are now being plunged back into the archaeopsychic past, uncovering the ancient taboos and drives that have been dormant for epochs. The brief span of an individual life is misleading. Each one of us is as old as the entire biological kingdom, and our bloodstreams are tributaries of the great sea of its total memory. The uterine odyssey of the growing foetus recapitulates the entire evolutionary past, and its central nervous system is a coded time scale, each nexus of neurones and each spinal level marking a symbolic station, a unit of neuronic time.

'The further down the CNS you move, from the hind-brain through the medulla into the spinal cord, you descend back into the neuronic past. For example, the junction between the thoracic and lumbar vertebrae, between T-12 and L-1, is the great zone of transit between the gill-breathing fish and the air-breathing amphibians with their respiratory rib-cages, the very junction where we stand now on the shores of this lagoon, between the Paleozoic and Triassic Eras.'

Bodkin moved back to his desk, and ran his hand over the rack of records. Listening distantly to Bodkin's quiet, unhurried voice, Kerans toyed with the notion that the row of parallel black discs was a model of a neurophonic spinal column. He remembered the faint drumming emitted by the record-player in Hardman's cabin, and its strange undertones. Perhaps the conceit was closer to the truth than he imagined?

Bodkin went on: 'If you like, you could call this the Psychology of Total Equivalents—let's say "Neuronics" for short—and dismiss it as metabiological fantasy. However, I am convinced that as we move back through geophysical time so we re-enter the amnionic corridor and move back through spinal and archaeopsychic time, recollecting in our unconscious minds the landscapes of each epoch, each with a distinct geological terrain, its own unique flora and fauna, as recognisable to anyone else as they would be to a traveller in a Wellsian time machine. Except that this is no scenic railway, but a total reorientation of the personality. If we let these buried phantoms master us as they re-appear we'll be swept back helplessly in the flood-tide like pieces of flotsam.' He picked one of the records from the rack, then pushed it away with a gesture of uncertainty. 'This afternoon I may have been taking a risk with Hardman, using the heater to simulate the sun and raise the temperature well into the 120's, but it was worth a chance. For the previous three weeks his dreams were almost driving him out of his mind, but during the last few days he's been much less disturbed, almost as if he were accepting the dreams and allowing himself to be carried back without retaining any conscious control. For his own sake I want to keep him awake as long as possible—the alarm clocks may do it.'

'If he remembers to keep them set,' Kerans commented quietly.

Outside in the lagoon the sounds of Riggs' cutter droned past. Stretching his legs, Kerans walked over to the window, and watched the landing craft swing in a diminishing arc around the base. While it berthed by the jetty Riggs held an informal conference with Macready across the gangway. Several times he pointed to the testing station with his baton, and Kerans assumed that they were preparing to tow the station over to the base. But for some reason the imminent departure left him unmoved. Bod-

kin's speculations, however nebulous, and his new psychology of
Neuronics, offered a more valid explanation for the metamorphosis taking place in his mind than any other. The tacit assumption
made by the UN directorate—that within the new perimeters
described by the Arctic and Antarctic Circles life would continue
much as before, with the same social and domestic relationships,
by and large the same ambitions and satisfactions—was obviously fallacious, as the mounting flood-water and temperature
would show when they reached the so-called polar redoubts. A
more important task than mapping the harbours and lagoons of
the external landscape was to chart the ghostly deltas and luminous beaches of the submerged neuronic continents.

'Alan,' he asked over his shoulder, still watching Riggs stamp-
ing about on the landing jetty, 'why don't you draft a report to
Byrd? I think you should let them know. There's always a chance
of—'

But Bodkin had gone. Kerans listened to his feet clump slowly
up the stairway and disappear into his cabin, the fatigued tread
of a man too old and too experienced to care whether or not his
warnings were heeded.

Kerans went back to his desk and sat down. From his jacket
pocket he withdrew the compass and placed it in front of him,
cradling it between his hands. Around him the muted sounds
of the laboratory formed a low background to his mind, the
furry puttering of the marmoset, the tick of a recording spool
somewhere, the grating of a revolving rig estimating a creeper's
phototropism.

Idly Kerans examined the compass, swinging the bearing
gently in its air-bath and then aligning the pointer and scale. He
tried to decide why he had taken it from the armoury. Normally
it was installed in one of the motor launches, and its disappearance would soon be reported, probably involve him in the petty
humiliation of admitting its theft.

Caging the compass, he rotated it towards himself, without

realising it sank into a momentary reverie in which his entire consciousness became focused on the serpentine terminal touched by the pointer, on the confused, uncertain but curiously potent image summed up by the concept 'South', with all its dormant magic and mesmeric power, diffusing outwards from the brass bowl held in his hands like the heady vapours of some spectral grail.

4

THE CAUSEWAYS OF THE SUN

THE NEXT DAY, for reasons Kerans was fully to understand
only much later, Lieutenant Hardman disappeared.

After a night of deep, dreamless sleep Kerans rose early and
had breakfasted by seven o'clock. He then spent an hour on the
balcony, sitting back in one of the beach chairs in a pair of white
latex shorts, the sunlight expanding across the dark water bathing his lean ebony body. Overhead the sky was vivid and mar-
bled, the black bowl of the lagoon, by contrast, infinitely deep
and motionless, like an immense well of amber. The tree-covered
buildings emerging from its rim seemed millions of years old,
thrown up out of the Earth's magma by some vast natural cat-
aclysm, embalmed in the gigantic intervals of time that had
elapsed during their subsidence.

Pausing by the desk to run his fingers over the brass compass gleaming in the darkness of the suite, Kerans went into
the bedroom and changed into his khaki drill uniform, a minimal concession to Riggs' preparations for departure. The Italian
sportswear was now hardly de rigueur, and it would only rouse
the Colonel's suspicions if he were seen sauntering about in a
pastel-coloured ensemble with a Ritz hallmark.

Although he accepted the possibility that he would remain

behind, Kerans found himself reluctant to make any systematic precautions. Apart from his fuel and food supplies, for which he had been dependent during the previous six months on Colonel Riggs' largesse, he had also needed an endless succession of minor spares and replacements, from a new watchface to a complete re-wiring of the lighting system in the suite. Once the base and its workshop had left he would soon find himself saddled with an accumulating series of petty annoyances, and with no accommodating technical sergeant to remove them.

For the convenience of the stores staff, and to save himself unnecessary journeys to and from the base, Kerans had stockpiled a month's forward supplies of canned food in the suite. Most of this consisted of condensed milk and luncheon meat, virtually inedible unless supplemented by the delicacies stored away in Beatrice's deep freeze. It was this capacious locker, with its reserves of pâté de foie gras and filet mignon, which Kerans counted upon to keep them going, but at the most there was a bare three month's stock. After that they would have to live off the land, switch their menu to wood soup and steak iguana.

Fuel raised more serious problems. The reserve tanks of diesel oil at the Ritz held little more than 500 gallons, sufficient to operate the cooling system for at most a couple of months. By closing down the bedroom and dressing room and moving into the lounge, and by raising the ambient temperature to ninety degrees, he would with luck double its life, but once the supplies were exhausted the chances of supplementing them were negligible. Every reserve tank and cache in the gutted buildings around the lagoons had long since been siphoned dry by the waves of refugees moving northward during the past thirty years in their power boats and cabin cruisers. The tank on the catamaran outboard motor carried three gallons, enough for thirty miles, or a return trip a day for a month between the Ritz and Beatrice's lagoon.

For some reason, however, this inverted Crusoeism—the

deliberate marooning of himself without the assistance of a gear-
laden carrack wrecked on a convenient reef—raised few anxie-
ties in Kerans' mind. As he let himself out of the suite he left the
thermostat at its usual eighty-degree setting, despite the fuel the
generator would waste, reluctant to make even a nominal concession to the hazards facing him after Riggs' departure. At first
he assumed that this reflected a shrewd unconscious assessment
that his good sense would prevail, but as he started the outboard
and drove the catamaran through the cool oily swells towards
the creek into the next lagoon he realised that this indifference
marked the special nature of the decision to remain behind. To
use the symbolic language of Bodkin's schema, he would then
be abandoning the conventional estimates of time in relation to
his own physical needs and entering the world of total, neuronic
time, where the massive intervals of the geological time-scale
calibrated his existence. Here a million years was the short-
est working unit, and problems of food and clothing became as
irrelevant as they would have been to a Buddhist contemplative
lotus-squatting before an empty rice-bowl under the protective
canopy of the million-headed cobra of eternity.

Entering the third lagoon, an oar raised to fend off the ten-
foot-long blades of a giant horse-tail dipping its leaves into the
mouth of the creek, he noticed without emotion that a party of
men under Sergeant Macready had hoisted the anchors of the
testing station and were towing it slowly towards the base. As the
gap between the two closed, like curtains drawing together after
the end of a play, Kerans stood in the stern of the catamaran
under the dripping umbrella of leaves, a watcher in the wings
whose contribution to the drama, however small, had now completely ended.

In order not to attract attention by re-starting the engine, he
pushed out into the sunlight, the giant leaves sinking to their
hilts in the green jelly of the water, and paddled slowly around
the perimeter of the lagoon to Beatrice's apartment block. Inter-

mittently the roar of the helicopter dinned across the water as
it carried out its tarmac check, and the swells from the testing
station drummed against the prows of the catamaran and drove
on through the open windows on his right, slapping around the
internal walls. Beatrice's power cruiser creaked painfully at its
moorings. The engine room had flooded and the stern was awash
under the weight of the two big Chrysler engines. Sooner or later
one of the thermal storms would catch the craft and anchor it
forever fifty feet down in one of the submerged streets.

When he stepped out of the elevator the patio around the
swimming pool was deserted, the previous evening's glasses still
on the tray between the reclining chairs. Already the sunlight
was beginning to fill the pool, illuminating the yellow sea-horses
and blue tridents that patterned its floor. A few bats hung in the
shadows below the gutter over Beatrice's bedroom window, but
they flew off as Kerans sat down, like vampiric spirits fleeing the
rising day.

Through the blinds Kerans caught a glimpse of Beatrice moving about quietly, and five minutes later she walked into the
lounge, a black towel in a single twist around her midriff. She
was partly hidden in the dim light at the far end of the room,
and seemed tired and withdrawn, greeting him with a half-
hearted wave. Leaning one elbow against the bar, she made
a drink for herself, stared blankly at one of the Delvaux and
returned to her bedroom.

When she failed to reappear Kerans went in search of her.
As he pushed back the glass doors the hot air trapped inside the
lounge hit his face like fumes vented from a crowded galley.
Several times within the past month the generator had failed
to respond immediately to the thermostat, and the temperature
was well into the nineties, probably responsible for Beatrice's
lethargy and ennui.

She was sitting on the bed when Kerans entered, the tumbler
of whiskey resting on her smooth knees. The thick hot air in the

room reminded Kerans of Hardman's cabin during the experiment Bodkin had conducted on the pilot. He went to the thermostat on the bedside table and jerked the tab down from seventy to sixty degrees.

'It's broken down again,' Beatrice told him matter-of-factly. 'The engine kept stopping.'

Kerans tried to take the glass from her hands but she steered it away from him. 'Leave me alone, Robert,' she said in a tired voice. 'I know I'm a loose, drunken woman, but I spent last night in the time jungles and I don't want to be lectured.'

Kerans scrutinised her closely, smiling to himself in a mixture of affection and despair. 'I'll see if I can repair the motor. This bedroom smells as if you've had an entire penal battalion billeted with you. Take a shower, Bea, and try to pull yourself together. Riggs is leaving tomorrow, we'll need our wits about us. What are these nightmares you're having?'

Beatrice shrugged. 'Jungle dreams, Robert,' she murmured ambiguously. 'I'm learning my ABC again. Last night was the delta jungles.' She gave him a bleak smile, then added with a touch of malicious humour: 'Don't look so stern, you'll be dreaming them too, soon.'

'I hope not.' Kerans watched distastefully as she raised the glass to her lips. 'And pour that drink away. Scotch breakfasts may be an old Highland custom, but they're murder on the liver.'

Beatrice waved him away. 'I know. Alcohol kills slowly, but I'm in no hurry. Go away, Robert.'

Kerans gave up and turned on his heel. He took the stairway from the kitchen into the store-room below, found a torch and the tool-set, and began to work on the generator.

HALF AN HOUR later, when he emerged on to the patio, Beatrice had apparently recovered completely from her torpor and was intently painting her nails with a bottle of blue varnish.

'Hello, Robert, are you in a better mood now?'

Kerans sat down on the tiled floor, wiping the last traces of grease off his hands. Crisply he punched the firm swell of her calf, then fended away the revenging heel at his head. 'I've cured the generator; with luck you won't have any more trouble. It's rather amusing; the timing device on the two-stroke starting engine had gone wrong, it was actually running backwards.'

He was about to explain the irony of the joke at full length when a loud-hailer blared from the lagoon below. The sounds of sudden excited activity had sprung up from the base; engines whined and accelerated, davits shrilled as the two reserve motor launches were lowered into the water, there was a medley of voices shouting and feet racing down gangways.

Kerans rose and hurried around the pool to the rail. 'Don't tell me they're leaving today—? Riggs is clever enough to try that in the hope of catching us unprepared.'

Beatrice at his side, the towel clasped to her breasts, they looked down at the base. Every member of the unit appeared to have been mobilised, and the cutter and the two launches surged and jockeyed around the landing jetty. The drooping rotors of the helicopter were circling slowly, Riggs and Macready about to embark. The other men were lined up on the jetty, waiting their turn to climb into the three craft. Even Bodkin had been roused from his bunk, and was standing bare-chested on the bridge of the testing station, shouting up at Riggs.

Suddenly Macready noticed Kerans at the balcony rail. He spoke to the Colonel, who picked up an electric megaphone and walked forwards across the roof.

'KER-ANS!! DOC-TOR KER-ANS!!'

Giant fragments of the amplified phrases boomed among the rooftops, echoing off the aluminium in-falls set into the sheets of windows. Kerans cupped his ears, trying to distinguish what the Colonel was shouting, but the sounds were lost in the mounting roar of the helicopter. Then Riggs and Macready climbed into the cabin, and the pilot began to semaphore at Kerans through the cockpit windscreen.

Kerans translated the morse signals, then turned quickly from the rail and began to carry the deck-chairs into the lounge.

'They're going to pick me up here,' he told Beatrice as the helicopter rose from its pedestal and lifted diagonally across the lagoon. 'You'd better get dressed or out of sight. The slip-steam will strip your towel away like tissue paper. Riggs has got enough to contend with now.'

Beatrice helped him furl the awning, and stepped into the lounge as the flickering shadow of the helicopter filled the patio, the down-draught fanning across their shoulders.

'But what's happened, Robert? Why is Riggs so excited?'

Kerans shielded his head from the engine roar and stared out across the green-ringed lagoons stretching towards the horizon, a sudden spasm of anxiety twisting one corner of his mouth.

'He's not excited, just worried stiff. Everything is beginning to collapse around him. Lieutenant Hardman has disappeared!'

LIKE AN IMMENSE putrescent sore, the jungle lay exposed below the open hatchway of the helicopter. Giant groves of gymnosperms stretched in dense clumps along the rooftops of the submerged buildings, smothering the white rectangular outlines. Here and there an old concrete water tower protruded from the morass, or the remains of a makeshift jetty still floated beside the hulk of a collapsing office block, overgrown with feathery acacias and flowering tamarisks. Narrow creeks, the canopies overhead turning them into green-lit tunnels, wound away from the larger lagoons, eventually joining the six hundred-yard-wide channels which broadened outwards across the former suburbs of the city. Everywhere the silt encroached, shoring itself in huge banks against a railway viaduct or crescent of offices, oozing through a submerged arcade like the fetid contents of some latter-day Cloaca Maxima. Many of the smaller lakes were now filled by the silt, yellow discs of fungus-covered sludge from which a profuse tangle of competing plant forms emerged, walled gardens in an insane Eden.

Clamped securely to the cabin handrail by the nylon harness around his waist and shoulders, Kerans gazed down at the unfolding landscape, following the waterways unwinding from the three central lagoons. Five hundred feet below, the shadow of the helicopter raced across the mottled green surface of the water, and he focused his attention on the area immediately around it. An immense profusion of animal life filled the creeks and canals: water-snakes coiled themselves among the crushed palisades of the water-logged bamboo groves, colonies of bats erupted out of the green tunnels like clouds of exploding soot, iguanas sat motionlessly on the shaded cornices like stone sphinxes. Often, as if disturbed by the noise of the helicopter, a human form seemed to dart and hide among the water-line windows, then revealed itself to be a crocodile snapping at a water-fowl, or one end of a subsiding log dislodged from the buffeted tree-ferns.

Twenty miles away the horizon was still obscured by the early morning mists, huge palls of golden vapour that hung from the sky like diaphanous curtains, but the air over the city was clear and vivid, the exhaust vapour of the helicopter sparkling as it receded in a long undulating signature. As they moved away from the central lagoons in their outward spiral sweep Kerans leaned against the hatchway and watched the glistening display, abandoning his search of the jungle below.

The chances of seeing Hardman from the air were infinitesimal. Unless he had taken refuge in a building near the base he would have been forced to travel along the water-ways, where he had the maximum possible protection from aerial observation under the overhanging fern trees.

In the starboard hatchway Riggs and Macready continued their vigil, passing a pair of binoculars to and fro. Without his peaked cap, his thin sandy hair blown forwards over his face,

Riggs looked like a ferocious sparrow, his little jaw jutting fiercely at the open air.

He noticed Kerans gazing up at the sky and shouted: 'Seen him yet, Doctor? Don't dawdle now, the secret of a successful sweep is one hundred percent cover, one hundred percent concentration.'

Accepting the rebuke, Kerans scanned the tilting disc of the jungle again, the tall towers of the central lagoon pivoting around the hatchway. Hardman's disappearance had been discovered by a sick-bay orderly at 8 o'clock that morning, but his bed was cold and he had almost certainly left the previous evening, probably soon after the final ward-roll at 9.30. None of the smaller scows hitched to the jetty rail had gone, but Hardman could easily have lashed together a couple of the empty fuel drums stored in a pile by the C-Deck hold and lowered them noiselessly into the water. However crude, such a craft would paddle smoothly and carry him ten miles away by day-break, somewhere on the perimeter of a search area of some seventy-five square miles, every acre of which was honeycombed by derelict buildings.

Unable to see Bodkin before being winched aboard the helicopter, Kerans could only speculate about Hardman's motives for leaving the base, and whether these were part of a grander design maturing slowly in the Lieutenant's mind or merely a sudden meaningless reaction to the news that they were leaving the lagoons for the north. Kerans' initial excitement had evaporated, and he felt a curious sense of relief, as if one of the opposing lines of force that encircled him had been removed by Hardman's disappearance and the tension and impotence contained in the system suddenly released. If anything, however, the task of remaining behind would now be even more difficult.

Unshackling his harness, Riggs stood up with a gesture of exasperation and handed the binoculars to one of the two soldiers squatting on the floor at the rear of the cabin.

'Open searches are a waste of time over this type of terrain,' he

shouted at Kerans. 'We'll go down somewhere and have a careful look at the map, you can have a shot at reading Hardman's
psychology.'

They were about ten miles north-west of the central lagoons,
the towers almost obscured in the mists along the horizon. Five
miles away, directly between them and the base, was one of the
two motor launches, cruising down an open channel, its white
wake fading across the glassy sheet of the water. Blocked by
the urban concentration to the south, less silt had penetrated
into the area, and the vegetation was lighter, more expanses of
unbroken water between the principal lines of buildings. Altogether the zone below them was empty and uncongested, and
Kerans felt convinced, though for no rational reason, that Hardman would not be found in the north-west sector.

Riggs climbed up into the cockpit and a moment later the
speed and inclination of the helicopter altered. They began to
make a shallow dive, swinging down to within a hundred feet of
the water, glided in and out of the wide canals looking for a convenient roof-top on which to perch. Finally they picked out the
humped back of a half-submerged cinema and let down slowly
on to the square firm roof of the neo-Assyrian portico.

For a few minutes they steadied their legs, gazing out over the
expanses of blue water. The nearest structure was an isolated
department store two hundred yards away, and the open vistas
reminded Kerans of Herodotus' description of the landscape in
Egypt at floodtime, with its rampart cities like the islands of the
Aegean Sea.

Riggs opened his map wallet and spread the polythene print
across the cabin floor. Resting his elbows on the edge of the
hatchway, he put his finger on their present landing stage.

'Well, Sergeant,' he told Daley, 'we seem to be half-way back
to Byrd. Apart from wearing out the engine we haven't achieved
much.'

Daley nodded, his small serious face hidden inside the fibreglass helmet. 'Sir, I think our only chance is to carry out low-level inspections over a few selected runs. There's just a hope we might see something—a raft or an oil patch.'

'Agreed. But the problem is'—here Riggs drummed on the map with his baton—'where? Hardman is very probably no more than two or three miles from the base. What's your guess, Doctor?'

Kerans shrugged. 'I don't really know what Hardman's motives are, Colonel. Latterly he'd been in Bodkin's charge. It may be . . .'

His voice began to trail off, and Daley cut in with another suggestion, distracting Riggs' attention. For the next five minutes the Colonel, Daley and Macready argued about possible routes Hardman had taken, marking only the wider water-ways as if Hardman were navigating a pocket battleship. Kerans looked around at the water eddying slowly past the cinema. A few branches and clumps of weed drifted along on the northward current, the bright sunlight masking the molten mirror of the surface. The water drummed against the portico beneath his feet, beating slowly against his mind, and setting up a widening circle of interference patterns as if crossing it at an opposite direction to its own course of flow. He watched a succession of wavelets lapping at the sloping roof, wishing that he could leave the Colonel and walk straight down into the water, dissolve himself and the ever-present phantoms which attended him like sentinel birds in the cool bower of its magical calm, in the luminous, dragon-green, serpent-haunted sea.

Suddenly he realised without any shadow of doubt where Hardman was to be found.

He waited for Daley to finish. '. . . I knew Lieutenant Hardman, sir, flew nearly five thousand hours with him, he's obviously had a brain-storm. He wanted to get back to Byrd, must have decided he couldn't wait any longer, not even two days. He'll have headed north, be resting somewhere along these open channels out of the city.'

Riggs nodded doubtfully, apparently unconvinced but prepared to accept the Sergeant's advice in default of any other.

'Well, you may be right. I suppose it's worth trying. What do
you think, Kerans?'

Kerans shook his head. 'Colonel, it's a complete waste of time
searching the areas north of the city. Hardman wouldn't have
come up here; it's too open and isolated. I don't know whether he's
on foot or paddling a raft, but he certainly isn't going north—Byrd
is the last place on Earth he wants to return to. There's only one
direction in which Hardman is heading—south.' Kerans pointed
to the nexus of channels which flowed into the central lagoons,
tributaries of a single huge water-way three miles south of the
city, its passage indented and diverted by the giant silt banks.
'Hardman will be somewhere along there. It probably took him
all night to reach the main channel, and I should guess that he's
resting in one of the small inlets before he moves on tonight.'

He broke off and Riggs stared hard at the map, peaked cap
pulled down over his eyes in a gesture of concentration.

'But why south?' Daley protested. 'Once he leaves the channel
there's nothing but solid jungle and open sea. The temperature is
going up all the time—he'll *fry*.'

Riggs looked up at Kerans. 'Sergeant Daley has a point, Doctor. Why should Hardman choose to travel south?'

Looking out across the water again, Kerans replied in a flat
voice: 'Colonel, there isn't any other direction.'

Riggs hesitated, then glanced at Macready, who had stepped
back from the group and was standing beside Kerans, his
tall stooped figure silhouetted like a gaunt crow against the
water. Almost imperceptibly he nodded to Riggs, answering
the unspoken question. Even Daley put a foot up on the cockpit entry step, accepting the logic of Kerans' argument and the
shared understanding of Hardman's motives once Kerans had
made them explicit.

Three minutes later the helicopter was speeding off at full
manifold pressure towards the lagoons in the south.

———

AS KERANS HAD PROPHESIED, they found Hardman among the silt flats.

Descending to three hundred feet above the water, they began to rake up and down the distal five-mile length of the main channel. The huge banks of silt lifted above the surface like the backs of yellow sperm whales. Wherever the hydrodynamic contours of the channel gave the silt banks any degree of permanence, the surrounding jungle spilled from the rooftops and rooted itself in the damp loam, matting the whole morass into an immovable structure. From the hatchway Kerans scrutinised the narrow beaches under the outer edge of the fern trees, watching for the tell-tale signs of a camouflaged raft or makeshift hut.

After twenty minutes, however, and a dozen careful sweeps of the channel, Riggs turned from the hatchway with a rueful shake of his head.

'You're probably right, Robert, but it's a hopeless job. Hardman's no fool, if he wants to hide from us we'll never find him. Even if he were leaning out of a window and waving, ten to one we wouldn't see him.'

Kerans murmured in reply, watching the surface below. Each of the tracking runs was about a hundred yards to the starboard of the previous one, and for the last three runs he had been watching the semicircular crescent of what appeared to be a large apartment block standing in the angle between the channel and the southern bank of a small creek which ran off into the surrounding jungle. The upper eight or nine storeys of the block stood above the water, enclosing a low mound of muddy-brown silt. The surface streamed with water draining away from a collection of shallow pools covering it. Two hours earlier the bank had been a sheet of wet mud, but by ten o'clock, as the helicopter flew over, the mud was beginning to dry and grow firm. To Kerans, shielding his eyes from the reflected sunlight, its smooth surface appeared to be scored by two faint parallel lines, about six feet apart, that led across to the jutting roof of an almost submerged balcony. As they swept overhead he tried to see under the concrete slab, but its mouth was choked with refuse and rotting logs.

He touched Riggs' arm and pointed to the tracks, so immersed in tracing their winding progress to the balcony that he almost failed to notice the equally distinct pattern of imprints emerging in the drying surface between the lines, spaced some four feet apart, unmistakably the footsteps of a tall powerful man hauling a heavy load.

AS THE NOISE of the helicopter's engine faded out on the roof above them, Riggs and Macready bent down and inspected the crude catamaran hidden behind a screen of bocage under the balcony. Fashioned from two drop-tanks lashed to either end of a metal bed-frame, its twin grey hulls were still streaked with silt. Clumps of mud from Hardman's feet crossed the room opening on to the balcony and disappeared through the suite into the adjacent corridor.

'This is it without a doubt—agree, Sergeant?' Riggs asked, stepping out into the sunlight to look up at the crescent of apartment blocks. A chain of autonomous units, they were linked by short causeways between the elevator wells at the end of each building. Most of the windows were broken, the cream facing tiles covered by huge patches of fungus, and the whole complex looked like an over-ripe camembert cheese.

Macready knelt down by one of the hulls, cleaning away the silt, then traced out the code number painted across the bow. 'UNAF 22-H-549—that's us, sir. The drop tanks were being cleared out yesterday, we'd stored them on C-Deck. He must have taken a spare bed from the sick-bay after ward-roll.'

'Good.' Rubbing his hands together with pleasure, Riggs stepped over to Kerans, smiling jauntily, his self-confidence and

good humour fully restored. 'Excellent, Robert. Superb diagnos-
tic skill. You were quite right, of course.' He peered shrewdly at
Kerans, as if speculating on the real sources of this remarkable
insight, invisibly marking him off. 'Cheer up, Hardman will be
grateful to you when we take him back.'

Kerans stood on the edge of the balcony, the slope of caking
silt below him. He looked up at the silent curve of windows, wondering which of the thousand or so rooms would be Hardman's
hiding-place. 'I hope you're right. You've still got to catch him.'

'Don't worry. We will.' Riggs began to shout up at the two men
on the roof, helping Daley lash down the helicopter. 'Wilson,
keep a look-out from the south-west end; Caldwell, you work your
way across to the north. Keep an eye on both sides, he might try
to swim for it.'

The two men saluted and moved off, their carbines held at
their hips. Macready cradled a Thompson gun in the crook of his
arm, and as Riggs unbuttoned the flap of his holster Kerans said
quietly: 'Colonel, we're not tracking down a wild dog.'

Riggs waved this aside. 'Relax, Robert, it's just that I don't
want my leg bitten off by some sleeping croc. Though as a matter of interest'—here he flashed Kerans a gleaming smile—
'Hardman has got a .45 Colt with him.'

Leaving Kerans to digest this, he picked up the electric
megaphone.

'Hardman! ! This is Colonel Riggs! !' He bellowed Hardman's
name at the silent heat, then winked at Kerans and added: *'Dr.
Kerans wants to talk to you, Lieutenant! !'*

Focused by the crescent of buildings, the sounds echoed away
across the swamps and creeks, booming distantly over the great
empty mudflats. Around them everything glistened in the
immense heat, and the men on the roof fretted nervously under
their forage caps. A thick cloacal stench exuded from the silt
flat, a corona of a million insects pulsing and humming hun-
grily above it, and a sudden spasm of nausea knotted Kerans'

gullet, for a moment dizzying him. Pressing a wrist tightly to his forehead, he leaned back against a pillar, listening to the echoes reverberate around him. Four hundred yards away two white-faced clock towers protruded through the vegetation, like the temple spires of some lost jungle religion, and the sounds of his name—'Kerans . . . Kerans . . . Kerans'—reflected off them seemed to Kerans to toll with an intense premonition of terror and disaster, the meaningless orientation of the clock hands identifying him, more completely than anything he had previously experienced, with all the confused and minatory spectres that cast their shadows more and more darkly through his mind, the myriad-handed mandala of cosmic time.

HIS NAME STILL ECHOED faintly in his ears as they began their search of the building. He took up his position at the stairwell at the centre of each corridor while Riggs and Macready inspected the apartments, keeping a look-out as they climbed the floors. The building had been gutted. All the floorboards had rotted or been ripped out, and they moved slowly along the tiled inlays, stepping warily from one concrete tie-beam to another. Most of the plaster had slipped from the walls and lay in grey heaps along the skirting boards. Wherever sunlight filtered through, the bare lathes were intertwined with creeper and wire-moss, and the original fabric of the building seemed solely supported by the profusion of vegetation ramifying through every room and corridor.

Through the cracks in the floors rose the stench of the greasy water swirling through the windows below. Disturbed for the first time in many years, the bats which hung from the tilting picture rails flew frantically for the windows, dispersing with cries of pain in the brilliant sunlight. Lizards scuttered and darted through the floor cracks, or skated desperately around the dry baths in the bathrooms.

Exacerbated by the heat, Riggs' impatience mounted as they

climbed the floors and had covered all but the top two without
success.

'Well, where is he?' Riggs rested against the stair-rail, gesturing for quiet, and listened to the silent building, breathing
tightly through his teeth. 'We'll stand easy for five minutes, Sergeant. Now's the time for caution. He's somewhere around here.'

Macready slung his Thompson over his shoulder and climbed
to the fan-light on the next landing which let in a thin breeze.
Kerans leaned against the wall, the sweat pouring across his
back and chest, temples thudding from the exertion of mounting the stairs. It was 11.30, and the temperature outside was well
over 120 degrees. He looked down at Riggs' flushed pink face,
admiring the Colonel's self-discipline and single-mindedness.

'Don't look so condescending, Robert. I know I'm sweating like
a pig, but I haven't had as much rest as you lately.'

The two men exchanged glances, each aware of the conflict
of attitude towards Hardman, and Kerans, in an effort to resolve
the rivalry between them, said quietly: 'You'll probably catch
him now, Colonel.'

Searching for somewhere to sit, he walked off down the corridor and pushed back the door into the first apartment.

As he unlatched the door the frame collapsed weakly into a
litter of worm-eaten dust and timbers, and he stepped across it
to the wide french windows overlooking the balcony. A little air
funnelled through, and Kerans let it play over his face and chest,
surveying the jungle below. The promontory on which the crescent of apartment houses stood had at one time been a small hill,
and a number of the buildings visible beneath the vegetation on
the other side of the silt flat were still above the flood-waters. Kerans stared at the two clock towers jutting up like white obelisks
above the fern fronds. The yellow air of the noon high seemed
to press down like a giant translucent counterpane on the leafy
spread, a thousand motes of light spitting like diamonds when-
ever a bough moved and deflected the sun's rays. The obscured

outline of a classical portico and colonnaded façade below the towers suggested that the buildings were once part of some small municipal centre. One of the clock-faces was without its hands; the other, by coincidence, had stopped at almost exactly the right time—11.35. Kerans wondered whether the clock was not in fact working, tended by some mad recluse clinging to a last meaningless register of sanity, though if the mechanism were still operable Riggs might well perform that role. Several times, before they abandoned one of the drowned cities, he had wound the two-ton mechanism of some rusty cathedral clock and they had sailed off to a last carillon of chimes across the water. For nights afterwards, in his dreams Kerans had seen Riggs dressed as William Tell, striding about in a huge Dalinian landscape, planting immense dripping sundials like daggers in the fused sand.

Kerans leaned against the window, waiting as the minutes passed and left behind the clock fixed at 11.35, overtaking it like a vehicle in a faster lane. Or was it not stationary (guaranteed though it would be to tell the time with complete, unquestionable accuracy twice a day—more than most time-pieces) but merely so slow that its motion *appeared* to be imperceptible? The slower a clock, the nearer it approximated to the infinitely gradual and majestic progression of cosmic time—in fact, by reversing a clock's direction and running it backwards one could devise a time-piece that in a sense was moving even more slowly than the universe, and consequently part of an even greater spatio-temporal system.

Kerans' amusement at this notion was distracted by his discovery among the clutter of debris on the opposite bank of a small cemetery sloping down into the water, its leaning headstones advancing to their crowns like a party of bathers. He remembered again one ghastly cemetery over which they had moored, its ornate Florentine tombs cracked and sprung, corpses floating out in their unravelling winding-sheets in a grim rehearsal of the Day of Judgement.

Averting his eyes, he turned away from the window, with a jolt realised that a tall black-bearded man was standing motionlessly in a doorway behind him. Startled, Kerans stared uncertainly at the figure, with an effort reassembling his thoughts. The big man stood in a slightly stooped but relaxed pose, his heavy arms loosely at his sides. Black mud caked across his wrists and forehead, and clogged his boots and the fabric of his drill trousers, for a moment reminding Kerans of one of the resurrected corpses. His bearded chin was sunk between his broad shoulders, the impression of constraint and fatigue heightened by the medical orderly's blue denim jacket several sizes too small which he wore, the corporal's stripe pulled up over the swell of his deltoid muscles. The expression on his face was one of hungry intensity, but he gazed at Kerans with sombre detachment, his eyes like heavily banked fires, a thin glow of interest in the biologist the only outward show of the energy within.

Kerans waited until his eyes adjusted themselves to the darkness at the rear of the room, looking involuntarily at the bedroom doorway through which the bearded man had stepped. He reached out one hand to him, half-afraid of breaking the spell between them, warning him not to move, and elicited in return an expression of curiously understanding sympathy, almost as if their roles were reversed.

'Hardman!' Kerans whispered.

With a galvanic leap, Hardman flung himself at Kerans, his big frame blocking off half the room, feinted just before they collided and swerved past, before Kerans could regain his balance had jumped out on to the balcony and climbed over the rail.

'*Hardman!*' As one of the men on the roof shouted the alarm Kerans reached the balcony. Hardman swung himself like an acrobat down the drain-pipe to the parapet below. Riggs and Macready dived into the room. Holding on to his hat, Riggs pivoted out over the rail, swore as Hardman disappeared into the apartment.

'Good man, Kerans. You nearly held him!' Together they ran

back into the corridor and raced down the stairway, saw Hardman swinging around the banisters four floors below, hurling himself from one landing to the next in a single stride.

When they reached the lowest floor they were thirty seconds behind Hardman, and a medley of excited shouts were coming from the roof. But Riggs paused stock-still on the balcony.

'Good God, he's trying to drag his raft back into the water!'

Thirty yards away, Hardman was dragging the catamaran across the caking mass of silt, the tow-rope over his shoulders, jerking its bows into the air with demoniac energy.

Riggs buttoned the flap of his holster, sadly shaking his head. There was a full fifty yards to the water's edge, and Hardman was sinking up to his knees in the damper silt, oblivious of the men on the roof looking down at him. Finally he tossed away the tow-rope and seized the bed-frame in both hands, began to wrench it along in slow painful jerks, the denim jacket splitting down his back.

Riggs stepped up on to the balcony, gesturing to Wilson and Caldwell to come down. 'Poor devil. He looks all in. Doctor, you stay close; you may be able to pacify him.'

Carefully they closed in on Hardman. The five men, Riggs, Macready, the two soldiers and Kerans, advanced down the sloping crust, shielding their eyes from the intense sunlight. Like a wounded water-buffalo, Hardman continued to wrestle in the mud ten yards in front of them. Kerans motioned to the others to stay still and then walked forwards with Wilson, a blond-haired youth who had once been Hardman's orderly. Wondering what to say to Hardman, he cleared the knots of phlegm from his throat.

On the roof behind them there was a sudden staccato roar of exhaust, splitting the silence of the tableau. A few steps behind Wilson, Kerans hesitated, saw Riggs look up in annoyance at the helicopter. Assuming that their mission was now over, Daley had started his engine, and the blades were swinging slowly through the air.

Roused from his attempt to reach the water, Hardman looked around at the group encircling him, released the catamaran and crouched down behind it. Wilson began to wade forward precariously through the soft silt along the water's edge, the carbine held across his chest. As he sank up to his waist he shouted at Kerans, his voice lost in the mounting roar of the engine, exhaust spitting in sharp cracks over their heads. Suddenly Wilson swayed, and before Kerans could steady him Hardman leaned across the catamaran, the big Colt .45 in his hand, and fired at them. The flame from the barrel stabbed through the dazzling air, and with a short cry Wilson fell across the carbine, then rolled back clutching a bloodied elbow, his forage cap cuffed off his head by the discharge wave of the explosion.

As the other men began to retreat up the slope Hardman holstered the revolver in his belt, turned and ran off along the water's edge to the buildings that merged into the jungle a hundred yards away.

Pursued by the ascending roar of the helicopter, they raced after Hardman, Riggs and Kerans helping the injured Wilson, stumbling in and out of the pot-holes left by the men ahead. At the edge of the silt flat the jungle rose in a high green cliff, tier upon tier of fern-trees and giant club moss flowering from the terraces. Without hesitating, Hardman plunged into a narrow interval between two ancient cobbled walls, and disappeared down the alley-way, Macready and Caldwell twenty yards behind him.

'Keep after him, Sergeant!' Riggs bellowed when Macready paused to wait for the Colonel. 'We've nearly got him; he's beginning to tire.' To Kerans he confided: 'God, what a shambles!' He pointed hopelessly at the huge figure of Hardman pounding away in long strides. 'What's driving the man on? I've a damn' good mind to let him go and get on with it.'

Wilson had recovered sufficiently to walk unaided, and Kerans left him and broke into a run. 'He'll be all right, Colonel. I'll try to talk to Hardman; there's a chance I may be able to hold him.'

From the alley-way they emerged into a small square, where a group of sedate 19th-century municipal buildings looked down on an ornate fountain. Wild orchids and magnolia entwined themselves around the grey ionic columns of the old courthouse, a miniature sham-Parthenon with a heavy sculptured portico, but otherwise the square had survived intact the assaults of the previous fifty years, its original floor still well above the surrounding water level. Next to the courthouse with the faceless clock tower, was a second colonnaded building, a library or museum, its white pillars gleaming in the sunlight like a row of huge bleached bones.

Nearing noon, the sun filled this antique forum with a harsh burning light, and Hardman stopped and looked back uncertainly at the men following him, then stumbled up the steps into the courthouse. Signalling to Kerans and Caldwell, Macready backed away among the statues in the square and took up his position behind the bowl of the fountain.

'Doctor, it's too dangerous now! He may not recognise you. We'll wait until the heat lifts; he can't move from there. Doctor—'

Kerans ignored him. He advanced slowly across the cracked flagstones, both forearms up over his eyes, and placed one foot insecurely on the first step. Somewhere among the shadows he could hear Hardman's exhausted breathing, pumping the scalding air into his lungs.

Shaking the square with its noise, the helicopter soared slowly overhead, and Riggs and Wilson hurried up the steps into the museum entrance, watching as the tail rotor turned the machine in a diminishing spiral. Together the noise and the heat drummed at Kerans' brain, bludgeoning him like a thousand clubs, clouds of dust billowing around him. Abruptly the helicopter began to lose lift, with an agonised acceleration of its engine slid out of the air into the square, then picked up just before it touched the ground. Ducking away, Kerans sheltered with Mac-

ready behind the fountain, while the aircraft jerked about over
their heads. As it revolved, the tail rotor lashed into the portico
of the courthouse, in an explosion of splintered marble the helicopter porpoised and plunged heavily on to the cobbles, the shattered tail propeller rotating eccentrically. Cutting his engine,
Daley sat back at his controls, half stunned by the impact with
the ground and trying helplessly to remove his harness.

FRUSTRATED AT THIS second attempt to catch Hardman, they
crouched in the shadows below the portico of the museum, waiting for the noon high to subside. As if illuminated by immense
searchlights, a vast white glare lit the grey stone of the buildings
around the square, like an over-exposed photograph, reminding
Kerans of the chalk-white colonnade of an Egyptian necropolis. As the sun mounted to its zenith the reflected light began to
glimmer upwards from the paving stones. Periodically, while he
tended Wilson and settled him with a few grains of morphine,
Kerans could see the other men as they kept up their watch for
Hardman, fanning themselves slowly with their forage caps.

Ten minutes later, shortly after noon, he looked up at the
square. Completely obscured by the light and glare, the buildings on the other side of the fountain were no longer continuously visible, looming in and out of the air like the architecture
of a spectral city. In the centre of the square, by the edge of the
fountain, a tall solitary figure was standing, the pulsing thermal
gradients every few seconds inverting the normal perspectives
and magnifying him fleetingly. Hardman's sun-burnt face and
black beard were now chalk-white, his mud-stained clothes glinting in the blinding sunlight like sheets of gold.

Kerans pulled himself to his knees, waiting for Macready to
leap forward at him, but the Sergeant, with Riggs beside him,
was huddled against a pillar, his eyes staring blankly at the floor
in front of them, as if asleep or entranced.

Stepping away from the fountain, Hardman moved slowly

across the square, in and out of the shifting curtains of light. He passed within twenty feet of Kerans, who knelt hidden behind the column, one hand on Wilson's shoulder, quietening the man's low grumbling. Skirting the helicopter, Hardman reached the far end of the courthouse and there left the square, walking steadily up a narrow incline towards the silt banks which stretched along the shore a hundred yards away.

Acknowledging his escape, the intensity of the sunlight diminished fractionally.

'Colonel Riggs!'

Macready plunged down the steps, shielding his eyes from the glare, and pointed off across the silt flat with his Thompson. Riggs followed him, hatless, his thin shoulders pinched together, tired and dispirited.

He put a restraining hand on Macready's elbow. 'Let him go, Sergeant. We'll never catch him now. There doesn't seem to be much point, anyway.'

Safely two hundred yards away, Hardman was still moving strongly, undeterred by the furnace-like heat. He reached the first crest, partly hidden in the huge palls of steam which hung over the centre of the silt flat, fading into them like a man disappearing into a deep mist. The endless banks of the inland sea stretched out in front of him, merging at their edges into the incandescent sky so that to Kerans he seemed to be walking across dunes of white-hot ash into the very mouth of the sun.

FOR THE NEXT two hours he sat quietly in the museum, waiting for the cutter to arrive, listening to Riggs' irritated grumbling and Daley's lame excuses. Drained by the heat, Kerans tried to sleep, but the occasional crack of a carbine jolted through his bruised brain like the kick of a leather boot. Attracted by the sounds of the helicopter, a school of iguana had approached, and the reptiles were now sidling around the edges of the square, braying at the men on the steps of the museum. Their harsh shrieking voices filled Kerans with a dull fear that persisted even after the cutter's arrival and their return journey to the base. Sitting in the comparative coolness under the wire hood, the green banks of the channel sliding past, he could hear their raucous barks.

At the base he settled Wilson in the sick-bay, then sought out Dr. Bodkin and described the events of the morning, referring in passing to the voices of the iguanas. Enigmatically, Bodkin only nodded to himself, then remarked: 'Be warned, Robert; you may hear them again.'

About Hardman's escape he made no comment.

Kerans' catamaran was still moored across the lagoon, so he decided to spend the night in his cabin at the testing station. There he passed a quiet afternoon, nursing a light fever in his bunk, thinking of Hardman and his strange southward odyssey, and of the silt banks glowing like luminous gold in the meridian sun, both forbidding and inviting, like the lost but forever beckoning and unattainable shores of the amnionic paradise.

5

DESCENT INTO DEEP TIME

LATER THAT NIGHT, as Kerans lay asleep in his bunk at the testing station, the dark waters of the lagoon outside drifting through the drowned city, the first of the dreams came to him. He had left his cabin and walked out on to the deck, looking down over the rail at the black luminous disc of the lagoon. Dense palls of opaque gas swirled across the sky only a few hundred feet overhead, through which he could just discern the faint glimmering outline of a gigantic sun. Booming distantly, it sent dull glows pulsing across the lagoon, momentarily lighting the long limestone cliffs which had taken the place of the ring of white-faced buildings.

Reflecting these intermittent flares, the deep bowl of the water shone in a diffused opalescent blur, the discharged light of myriads of phosphorescing animalcula, congregating in dense shoals like a succession of submerged haloes. Between them the water was thick with thousands of entwined snakes and eels, writhing together in frantic tangles that tore the surface of the lagoon.

As the great sun drummed nearer, almost filling the sky itself, the dense vegetation along the limestone cliffs was flung back abruptly, to reveal the black and stone-grey heads of enormous Triassic lizards. Strutting forward to the edge of the cliffs, they began to roar together at the sun, the noise gradually mounting until it became indistinguishable from the volcanic pounding of the solar flares. Kerans felt, beating within him like his own pulse, the powerful mesmeric pull of the baying reptiles, and stepped out into the lake, whose waters now seemed an extension of his own bloodstream. As the dull pounding rose, he felt the barriers which divided his own cells from the surrounding medium dissolving, and he swam forwards, spreading outwards across the black thudding water. . . .

HE WOKE IN THE suffocating metal box of his cabin, his head splitting like a burst marrow, too exhausted to open his eyes. Even as he sat on the bed, splashing his face in the luke-warm water from the jug, he could still see the vast inflamed disc of the spectral sun, still hear the tremendous drumming of its beat. Timing them, he realised that the frequency was that of his own heartbeats, but in some insane way the sounds were magnified so that they remained just above the auditory threshold, reverberating dimly off the metal walls and ceiling like the whispering murmur of some blind pelagic current against the hull-plates of a submarine.

The sounds seemed to pursue him as he opened the cabin door and moved down the corridor to the gallery. It was shortly after 6 a.m. and the testing station stirred with a faint hollowed silence, the first flares of the false dawn illuminating the dusty reagent benches and the crates stacked under the fan-lights in the corridor. Several times Kerans paused and tried to shrug off the echoes that persisted in his ears, uneasily wondering what was the real identity of his new pursuers. His unconscious was rapidly becoming a well-stocked pantheon of tutelary phobias and obsessions, homing on to his already over-burdened psyche like lost telepaths. Sooner or later the archetypes themselves would become restive and start fighting each other, anima against persona, ego against id. . . .

Then he remembered that Beatrice Dahl had seen the same
dream and pulled himself together. He went out on to the deck
and looked across the slack water of the lagoon at the distant
spire of the apartment block, trying to decide whether to borrow
one of the scows moored to the jetty and drive over to her. Having now experienced one of the dreams, he realised the courage
and self-sufficiency Beatrice had displayed, brushing off the least
show of sympathy.

And yet Kerans knew that for some reason he had been reluctant to give Beatrice any real sympathy, cutting his questions
about the nightmares as short as possible and never offering
her treatment or sedative. Nor had he tried to follow up any of
Bodkin's or Riggs' oblique remarks about the dreams and their
danger, almost as if he had known that he would soon be shar-
ing them, and accepted them as an inevitable element of his
life, like the image of his own death each of them carried with
him in the secret places of his heart. (Logically—for what had
a more gloomy prognosis than life?—every morning one should
say to one's friends: 'I grieve for your irrevocable death', as to
anyone suffering from an incurable disease, and was the universal omission of this minimal gesture of sympathy the model for
their reluctance to discuss the dreams?)

Bodkin was sitting at the table in the galley when Kerans
entered, placidly drinking coffee brewed in a large cracked
saucepan on the stove. His shrewd quick eyes watched Kerans
unobtrusively as he lowered himself into a chair and massaged
his forehead slowly with a febrile hand.

'So you're one of the dreamers now, Robert. You've beheld the
fata morgana of the terminal lagoon. You look tired. Was it a
deep one?'

Kerans managed a rueful laugh. 'Are you trying to frighten
me, Alan? I wouldn't know yet, but it felt deep enough. God, I
wish I hadn't spent last night here. There are no nightmares at
the Ritz.' He sipped pensively at the hot coffee. 'So that's what

Riggs was talking about. How many of his men are seeing these dreams?'

'Riggs himself doesn't, but at least half the others. And Beatrice Dahl, of course. I've been seeing them for a full three months. It's basically the same recurrent dream in all cases.' Bodkin spoke in a slow unhurried voice, with a softer tone than his usual blunt delivery, as if Kerans had now become a member of a select inner group. 'You've held out for a long time, Robert, it's quite a tribute to the strength of your preconscious filters. We were all beginning to wonder when you'd arrive.' He smiled at Kerans. 'Figuratively, of course. I've never discussed the dreams with anyone. Except for Hardman, and there, poor chap, the dreams were having him.' As an afterthought he added: 'You spotted the sun : pulse equation? Hardman's gramophone record was a play-back of his own pulse, amplified in the hope of precipitating the crisis then and there. Don't think I sent him out into those jungles deliberately.'

Kerans nodded and gazed out through the window at the rounded bulk of the floating base moored alongside. High up on the top deck Sergeant Daley, the helicopter co-pilot, was standing motionless by the rail, staring across the cool early morning water. Perhaps he too had just woken from the same corporate nightmare, was filling his eyes with the olive-green spectrum of the lagoon in the forlorn expectation of erasing the burning image of the Triassic sun. Kerans looked down at the dark shadows below the table, seeing again the faint glimmer of the phosphorescing pools. Distantly in his ears he could hear the sun drumming over the sunken water. As he recovered from his first fears he realised that there was something soothing about its sounds, almost reassuring and encouraging like his own heartbeats. But the giant reptiles had been terrifying.

He remembered the iguanas braying and lungeing across the steps of the museum. Just as the distinction between the latent and manifest contents of the dream had ceased to be valid, so had any division between the real and the super-real in the external world. Phantoms slid imperceptibly from nightmare to reality and back again, the terrestrial and psychic landscapes were now indistinguishable, as they had been at Hiroshima and Auschwitz, Golgotha and Gomorrah.

Sceptical of the remedy, he said to Bodkin: 'You'd better lend me Hardman's alarm clock, Alan. Or better still, remind me to take a phenobarbitone tonight.'

'Don't,' Bodkin warned him firmly. 'Not unless you want the impact doubled. Your residues of conscious control are the only thing holding up the dam.' He buttoned his cotton jacket around his shirtless chest. 'That wasn't a true dream, Robert, but an ancient organic memory millions of years old.'

He pointed to the ascending rim of the sun through the groves of gymnosperms. 'The innate releasing mechanisms laid down in your cytoplasm millions of years ago have been awakened, the expanding sun and the rising temperature are driving you back down the spinal levels into the drowned seas submerged beneath the lowest layers of your unconscious, into the entirely new zone of the neuronic psyche. This is the lumbar transfer, total biopsychic recall. We really *remember* these swamps and lagoons. After a few nights you won't be frightened of the dreams, despite their superficial horror. That's why Riggs has received orders for us to leave.'

'The Pelycosaur . . . ?' Kerans asked.

Bodkin nodded. 'The joke was on us. The reason they didn't take the report seriously at Byrd was that our's wasn't the first to be reported.'

FOOTSTEPS SOUNDED up the companionway and moved briskly along the metal deck outside. Colonel Riggs pushed back the double swing doors, freshly scrubbed and breakfasted.

He waved his baton at them amiably, eyeing the litter of unwashed cups and his two reclining subordinates.

'God, what a pig hole. Morning to you both. We've got a busy day ahead of us so let's get our elbows off the table. I've fixed the departure time for twelve hundred hours tomorrow, and there'll be a final embarkation stand-by at ten hundred. I don't want to waste any more fuel than I have to, so dump everything you can overboard. You all right, Robert?'

'Perfectly,' Kerans replied flatly, sitting up.

'Glad to hear it. You look a bit glassy. Right, then. If you want to borrow the cutter to evacuate the Ritz . . .'

Kerans listened to him automatically, watching the sun as it rose magnificently behind the gesticulating outline of the Colonel. What completely separated them now was the single fact that Riggs had not seen the dream, not felt its immense hallucinatory power. He was still obeying reason and logic, buzzing around his diminished, unimportant world with his little parcels of instructions like a worker bee about to return to the home nest. After a few minutes he ignored the Colonel completely and listened to the deep subliminal drumming in his ears, half-closed his eyes so that he could see the glimmering surface of the lake dapple across the dark underhang of the table.

Opposite him Bodkin appeared to be doing the same, his hands folded over his navel. During how many of their recent conversations had he in fact been miles away?

When Riggs left, Kerans followed him to the door. 'Of course, Colonel, everything will be ready in good time. Thank you for calling.'

As the cutter moved off across the lagoon he went back to his chair. For a few minutes the two men stared across the table at each other, the insects outside bouncing off the wire mesh as the sun lifted into the sky. At last Kerans spoke.

'Alan, I'm not sure whether I shall be leaving.'

Without replying, Bodkin took out his cigarettes. He lit one carefully, then sat back smoking it calmly. 'Do you know where we are?' he asked after a pause. 'The name of this city?' When

Kerans shook his head he said: 'Part of it used to be called London; not that it matters. Curiously enough, though, I was born here. Yesterday I rowed over to the old University quarter, a mass of little creeks, actually found the laboratory where my father used to teach. We left here when I was six, but I can just remember being taken to meet him one day. A few hundred yards away there was a planetarium, I saw a performance once—that was before they had to re-align the projector. The big dome is still there, about twenty feet below water. It looks like an enormous shell, fucus growing all over it, straight out of *The Water Babies*. Curiously, looking down at the dome seemed to bring my childhood much nearer. To tell the truth, I'd more or less forgotten it—at my age all you have are the memories of memories. After we left here our existence became completely nomadic, and in a sense this city is the only home I've ever known—' He broke off abruptly, his face suddenly tired.

'Go on,' Kerans said evenly.

6

THE DROWNED ARK

THE TWO MEN moved quickly along the deck, their padded soles soundless on the metal plates. A white midnight sky hung across the dark surface of the lagoon, a few stationary clumps of cumulus like sleeping galleons. The low night sounds of the jungle drifted over the water; occasionally a marmoset gibbered or the iguanas shrieked distantly from their eyries in the submerged office blocks. Myriads of insects festered along the waterline, momentarily disturbed as the swells rolled in against the base, slapping at the canted sides of the pontoon.

Kerans began to cast off the restraining lines one by one, taking advantage of the swells to lift the loops off the rusting bollards. As the station slowly pivoted away he looked up anxiously at the dark bulk of the base. Gradually the three nearside blades of the helicopter came into view above the top deck, then the slender tail rotor. He paused before releasing the last line, waiting for Bodkin to give the all-clear from the starboard bridge.

The tension on the line had doubled, and it took Kerans several minutes to work the metal loop up the curving lip of the bollard, the successive swells giving him a few inches of slack as the station tilted, followed a moment later by the base. Above him he could hear Bodkin whispering impatiently—they had swung right around into the narrow interval of water behind them and were now face on to the lagoon, the single light in Beatrice's penthouse burning on its pylon. Then he cleared the lip and lowered the heavy cable into the slack water three feet below, watching it cleave back towards the base.

Freed of its attendant burden, and with its centre of gravity raised by the helicopter on its roof, the huge drum rolled over a full five degrees from the vertical, then gradually regained its balance. A light in one of the cabins went on, then flicked off again after a few moments. Kerans seized the boat-hook on the deck beside him as the interval of open water widened, first to twenty yards, then to fifty. A low current moved steadily through the lagoons, and would carry them back along the shore to their former mooring.

Holding the station off from the buildings they skirted, now and then crushing the soft fern trees sprouting through the windows, they soon covered two hundred yards, slowing as the current diminished around the curve, and finally lodged in a narrow inlet about a hundred feet square in size.

Kerans leaned over the rail, looking down through the dark water at the small cinema theatre twenty feet below the surface, its flat roof luckily uncluttered by elevator-heads or fire escapes. Waving to Bodkin on the deck above, he stepped in through the laboratory and made his way past the specimen tanks and sinks to the companionway leading down to the float.

Only one stop-cock had been built into the base of the float, but as he turned the handwheel a powerful jet of cold foaming water gushed up around his legs. By the time he returned to the lower deck, to make a final check of the laboratory, water was already spilling ankle-deep through the scuppers, sluicing among the sinks and benches. He quickly released the marmoset from its fume cupboard and pushed the bushy-tailed mammal through one of the windows. The station went down like an elevator, and he waded waist-deep to the companionway and climbed up to the next deck where Bodkin was exultantly watching the windows of the adjacent office blocks rise into the air.

They settled about three feet below deck level, on a flat keel with a convenient access point by the starboard bridge. Dimly below they could hear trapped air bubbling from the retorts and glass-ware in the laboratory, and a frothy stain spread across the water from a submerged window by one of the reagent benches.

Kerans watched the indigo bubbles fade and dissolve, thinking of the huge semi-circle of programme charts sinking below the water as he left the laboratory, a perfect, almost vaudevillean comment on the biophysical mechanisms they sought to describe, and which perhaps symbolised the uncertainties that lay ahead now that he and Bodkin had committed themselves to remaining behind. They were now entering the *aqua incognita*, with only a few rule-of-thumb principles to guide them.

From the typewriter in his cabin Kerans took a sheet of paper, pinned it firmly to the door of the galley. Bodkin appended his signature to the message, and the two men went out on the deck again and lowered Kerans' catamaran into the water.

Paddling slowly, the outboard shipped, they glided off across the black water, soon disappearing among the dark blue shadows along the edge of the lagoon.

AS THE DOWN-DRAUGHT from its blades fanned furiously across the swimming pool, tearing at the striped awning of the patio, the helicopter circled deafeningly over the penthouse, plunging and diving as it searched for a landing point. Kerans smiled to himself as he watched it through the plastic vanes over the lounge windows, confident that the tottering pile of kerosene drums he and Bodkin had pyramided over the roof would safely deter the pilot. One or two of the drums toppled down on to the patio and splashed into the pool, and the helicopter veered away and then came in more slowly, hovering steadily.

The pilot, Sergeant Daley, swung the fuselage around so that the hatch door faced the lounge windows, and the hatless figure of Riggs appeared in the doorway, two of the soldiers holding on to him as he bellowed into an electric megaphone.

Beatrice Dahl ran across to Kerans from her observation post at the far end of the lounge, cupping her ears from the din.

'Robert, he's trying to talk to us!'

Kerans nodded, the Colonel's voice completely lost in the engine roar. Riggs finished and the helicopter leaned backwards and soared away across the lagoon, taking the noise and vibration with it.

Kerans put his arm around Beatrice's shoulders, the bare oiled skin smooth under his fingers. 'Well, I think we have a pretty good idea what he was saying.'

They went out on to the patio, waving up to Bodkin, who had appeared from the elevator-house and was straightening the drums. Below them, on the opposite side of the lagoon, the upper deck and bridge of the scuttled testing station protruded from the water, a flotsam of hundreds of pieces of old note-paper eddying away from it. Standing by the rail, Kerans pointed to the yellow hull of the base moored by the Ritz in the furthest of the three central lagoons.

After a futile attempt to re-float the station, Riggs had set off at noon as planned, sending the cutter over to the apartment house where he assumed the two biologists were hiding. Finding the elevator out of order, his men had refused the alternative of a twenty-storey climb up the stairway—already a few iguanas had made their homes on the lower landings—so Riggs had finally tried to reach them with the helicopter. Balked there, he was now crashing the Ritz.

'Thank God he's left,' Beatrice said fervently. 'For some reason he really got on my nerves.'

'You made that pretty plain. I'm surprised he didn't take a pot shot at you.'

'But, darling, he was insufferable. All that stiff upper lip stuff and dressing for dinner in the jungle—a total lack of adaptability.'

'Riggs was all right,' Kerans remarked quietly. 'He'll probably get by.' Now that Riggs had gone he was aware of how dependent he had been on the Colonel's buoyancy and good humour. Without him the morale of the unit would have disintegrated in an instant. It remained to be seen whether Kerans could imbue his own little trio with the same degree of confidence and sense of purpose. Certainly it was up to him to be the leader; Bodkin was too old, Beatrice too self-immersed.

Kerans glanced at the thermo-alarm he wore next to his wristwatch. It was after 3.30, but the temperature was still a hundred and ten degrees, the sun beating against his skin like a fist. They joined Bodkin and went into the lounge.

Resuming the action conference interrupted by the helicopter, Kerans said: 'You've got about a thousand gallons left in the roof tank, Bea, enough for three months—or let's say two as we can expect it to get a lot hotter—and I recommend you to close down the rest of the apartment and move into here. You're on the north side of the patio so the elevator-house will protect you from the heavy rains when they come in on the southerly storms. Ten to one the shutters and air-seals along the bedroom walls will be breached. What about food, Alan? How long will the stocks in the deep freeze last?'

Bodkin pulled a distasteful face. 'Well, as most of the lambs' tongues in aspic have been eaten they now consist chiefly of bully beef, so you could say 'indefinitely'. However, if you're actually planning to eat the stuff—six months. But I'd prefer iguana.'

'No doubt the iguana would prefer us. All right then, that seems pretty fair. Alan will be over in the station until the level rises, and I'll be holding out at the Ritz. Anything else?'

Beatrice wandered away around the sofa towards the bar.

'Yes, darling. Shut up. You're beginning to sound like Riggs. The military manner doesn't suit you.'

Kerans threw her a mock salute and strolled over to look at the painting by Ernst at the far end of the lounge, while Bodkin gazed down at the jungle through the window. More and more the two scenes were coming to resemble each other, and in turn the third nightscape each of them carried within his mind. They never discussed their dreams, the common zone of twilight where they moved at night like the phantoms in the Delvaux painting.

Beatrice had sat down on the sofa with her back to him, and shrewdly Kerans guessed that the present unity of the group would not be long maintained. Beatrice was right; the military manner did not suit him, his personality was too passive and introverted, too self-centred. More important, though, they were entering a new zone, where the usual obligations and allegiances ceased to operate. Now that they had made their decision the bonds between them had already begun to fade, and it was not simply for reasons of convenience that they would live apart. Much as he needed Beatrice Dahl, her personality intruded upon the absolute freedom he required for himself. By and large, each of them would have to pursue his or her own pathway through the time jungles, mark their own points of no return. Although they might see one another occasionally, around the lagoons or at the testing station, their only true meeting ground would be in their dreams.

7

CARNIVAL OF ALLIGATORS

SPLIT BY AN IMMENSE ROAR, the early morning silence over the lagoon shattered abruptly, and a tremendous blare of noise battered past the windows of the hotel suite. With an effort Kerans pulled his reluctant body from his bed and stumbled across the books scattered on the floor. He kicked back the mesh door on to the balcony in time to see a huge white-hulled hydroplane speed by around the lagoon, its two long stepped planes cleaving perfect slices of glittering spray. As the heavy wash slapped against the wall of the hotel, breaking up the colonies of water spiders and disturbing the bats nesting among the rotting logs, he caught a glimpse of a tall, broad-shouldered man in the cockpit, wearing a white helmet and jerkin, standing upright at the controls.

He drove the hydroplane with an easy nonchalant swagger, accelerating the two powerful propeller turbines mounted in front of him as the craft hit the broad swells across the lagoon, so that it plunged and dived like a power-boat wrestling through giant rollers, throwing up gales of rainbowing spray. The man rolled with the surging motion of the craft, his long legs supple and relaxed, like a charioteer completely in command of a spirited team.

Hidden by the calamites which now spilled across the balcony—the effort of cutting them back had long seemed pointless—Kerans watched him unobserved. As the craft sped by on its second circuit, Kerans had a glimpse of a rakish profile, bright eyes and teeth, an expression of exhilarated conquest.

The silver studs of a cartridge belt flashed around his waist, and when he reached the far side of the lagoon there was a series of short explosions. Signal shells burst over the water into ragged red umbrellas, the fragments spitting down across the shore.

In a final lunge of energy, its engines screaming, the hydroplane swerved out of the lagoon and gunned away down the canal to the next lagoon, its wash thrashing at the foliage. Kerans gripped the balcony rail, watching the disturbed restless water of the lagoon trying to re-settle itself, the giant cryptograms and scale trees along the shore tossed and flurried by the still surging air. A thin pall of red vapour drifted away to the north, fading with the diminishing sounds of the hydroplane. The violent irruption of noise and energy, and the arrival of this strange white-suited figure, momentarily disconcerted Kerans, jerking him roughly from his lassitude and torpor.

In the six weeks since Riggs' departure he had lived almost alone in his penthouse suite at the hotel, immersing himself more and more deeply in the silent world of the surrounding jungle. The continued increase in temperature—the thermo-alarm on the balcony now registered a noon high of one hundred and thirty degrees—and the enervating humidity made it almost impossible to leave the hotel after ten o'clock in the morning; the lagoons and the jungle were filled with fire until four o'clock, by when he was usually too tired to do anything but return to bed.

All day he sat by the shuttered windows of the suite, listening from the shadows to the shifting movement of the mesh cage, as it expanded and contracted in the heat. Already many of the buildings around the lagoon had disappeared beneath the proliferating vegetation; huge club-mosses and calamites blotted out the white rectangular faces, shading the lizards in their window lairs.

Beyond the lagoon the endless tides of silt had begun to accumulate in enormous glittering banks, here and there over-topping the shore-line, like the immense tippings of some distant gold-mine. The light drummed against his brain, bathing the submerged levels below his consciousness, carrying him downwards into warm pellucid depths where the nominal realities of time and space ceased to exist. Guided by his dreams, he was moving backwards through the emergent past, through a succession of ever stranger landscapes, centred upon the lagoon, each of which, as Bodkin had said, seemed to represent one of his own spinal levels. At times the circle of water was spectral and vibrant, at others slack and murky, the shore apparently formed of shale, like the dull metallic skin of a reptile. Yet again the soft beaches would glow invitingly with a glossy carmine sheen, the sky warm and limpid, the emptiness of the long stretches of sand total and absolute, filling him with an exquisite and tender anguish.

He longed for this descent through archaeopsychic time to reach its conclusion, repressing the knowledge that when it did the external world around him would have become alien and unbearable.

Sometimes he restlessly made a few entries in his botanical diary about the new plant forms, and during the first weeks called several times on Dr. Bodkin and Beatrice Dahl. But both were increasingly preoccupied with their own descents through total time. Bodkin had become lost in his private reverie, punting aimlessly around the narrow creeks in search of the submerged world of his childhood. Once Kerans came across him resting on an oar in the stern of his small metal scow and gazing vacantly at the unyielding buildings around him. He had stared straight through Kerans, failing to acknowledge his call.

However, with Beatrice, despite their superficial estrangement, there was an intact underlying union, a tacit awareness of their symbolic roles.

MORE SIGNAL SHELLS burst over the distal lagoon, containing
the station and Beatrice's apartment house, and Kerans shielded
his eyes as the bright fire-balls studded the sky. A few seconds
later, several miles away among the silt banks to the south, there
was a series of answering bursts, faint puffs that soon dispersed.

So the stranger driving the hydroplane was not alone. At
the prospect of this imminent invasion Kerans pulled himself
together. The distance separating the answering signals was
wide enough to indicate that there was more than one group, and
that the hydroplane was merely a scout vehicle.

Sealing the mesh door behind him, he stepped back into the
suite, pulling his jacket off the chair. Out of habit he went into
the bathroom and stood in front of the mirror, absently feeling
the week-old stubble on his face. The hair was white as pearl,
and with his ebony tan and introspective eyes gave him the
appearance of a refined and cultivated beachcomber. A bucketful
of dingy water had leaked in from the wrecked still on the roof,
and he scooped some out and splashed his face, a token toilet performed, as far as he could see, solely out of habit.

Using the metal-tipped boat-hook to drive away two small
iguanas idling on the jetty, he slid the catamaran into the water
and cast off, the little outboard carrying him steadily through
the sluggish swells. Huge clumps of algae stirred below the craft,
and stick-beetle and water spider raced around its prows. It was
a few minutes after seven o'clock, and the temperature was only
eighty degrees, comparatively cool and pleasant, the air free of
the enormous clouds of mosquitoes which would later be roused
from their nests by the heat.

As he navigated the hundred-yard-long creek leading into the
southern lagoon more signal rockets were exploding overhead,
and he could hear the hydroplane zooming to and fro, occasionally glimpse the white-suited figure at its controls as it flashed

past. Kerans cut the outboard at the entrance to the lagoon and glided quietly through the overhanging fern fronds, watching for water snakes disturbed from the branches by the surging wash.

Twenty-five yards along the shore he berthed the catamaran among the horse-tails growing on the shelving roof of a department store, waded up the sloping concrete to a fire escape on the side of the adjacent building. He climbed the five storeys to the flat roof-top and lay down behind a low pediment, glancing up at the nearby bulk of Beatrice's apartment house.

The hydroplane was circling noisily by an inlet on the far side of the lagoon, the driver plunging it backwards and forwards like a horseman reining his steed. More flares were going up, some only a quarter of a mile away. As he watched Kerans noticed a low but mounting roar, a harsh animal sound not unlike that emitted by the iguanas. It drew nearer, mingled with the drone of engines, followed by the noise of vegetation being torn and buffeted. Sure enough, along the course followed by the inlet, the huge fern trees and calamites were flung down one after the other, their branches waving as they fell like vanquished standards. The whole jungle was being torn apart. Droves of bats erupted into the air and scattered frantically across the lagoon, their screeching masked by the accelerating turbines of the hydroplane and the exploding star-shells.

Abruptly, the water in the mouth of the inlet rose several feet into the air, what seemed to be an enormous log-jam crushed down it, tearing the vegetation away, and burst out into the lagoon. A miniature niagara of foaming water cascaded outwards, impelled by the pressure of the tidal bore behind it, on which rode several square black-hulled craft similar to Colonel Riggs' cutter, paint peeling from the giant dragon eyes and teeth slashed across their bows. Manned by a dozen dusky-skinned figures in white shorts and singlets, the scows jockeyed out towards the centre of the lagoon, the last of the star-shells still going up from their decks in the general mêlée and excitement.

Half-deafened by the noise, Kerans stared down at the vast swarm of long brown forms swimming powerfully through the seething water, their massive tails lashing the foam. By far the largest alligators he had seen, many of them over twenty-five feet long, they jostled together ferociously as they fought their way into the clear water, churning in a pack around the now stationary hydroplane. The white-suited man was standing in the open hatchway, hands on hips, gazing exultantly at this reptilian brood. He waved lazily at the crews of the three scows, then gestured in a wide circle at the lagoon, indicating that they would anchor there.

As his Negro lieutenants re-started their engines and drifted off towards the bank, he surveyed the surrounding buildings with a critical eye, his strong face raised almost jauntily to one side. The alligators congregated like hounds around their master, the wheeling cries of the dense cloud of sentinel birds overhead, Nile plover and stone curlew, piercing the morning air. More and more of the alligators joined the pack, cruising shoulder to shoulder in a clock-wise spiral, until at least two thousand were present, a massive group incarnation of reptilian evil.

WITH A SHOUT, the pilot swung back to his controls, the two thousand snouts lifting in recognition. The propellers kicked into life and lifted the hydroplane forward across the water. Its sharp planes ploughing straight across the hapless creatures in their path, it drove away towards the communicating creek into the next lagoon, the great mass of alligators surging along behind it. A few detached themselves and cruised off in pairs around the lagoon, ferreting among the submerged windows and driving off the iguanas who had come out to watch. Others glided among the buildings and took up their positions on the barely covered roof-tops. Behind them, in the centre of the lagoon, the beaten water churned uneasily, occasionally throwing up the snow-white belly of a dead alligator crushed by the hydroplane.

As the advancing armada headed towards the creek on his left, Kerans scrambled down the fire escape and splashed down the sloping roof to the catamaran. Before he could reach it the heavy wash set up by the hydroplane had rocked the craft adrift, and it floated off into the oncoming mass. Within a few seconds it was engulfed, upended by the press of alligators fighting to get into the creek and cut to pieces in their snapping jaws.

A large caiman bringing up the rear spotted Kerans waist-deep among the horse-tails and veered towards him, its eyes steadying. Its rough scaly back and the crest along its tail flexed powerfully as it surged through the water. Quickly Kerans retreated up the slope, slipping once to his shoulders, reached the fire escape as the caiman lumbered out of the shallows on its short hooked legs and lunged at his leaping feet.

Panting, Kerans leaned on the rail, looking down at the cold unblinking eyes which regarded him dispassionately.

'You're a well-trained watchdog,' he told it ungrudgingly. He eased a loose brick from the wall and launched it with both hands at the knob on the end of the caiman's snout, grinning as it bellowed and backed off, snapping irritably at the horse-tails and a few drifting spars of the catamaran.

AFTER HALF AN HOUR, and a few minor duels with the retreating iguanas, he managed to cross the intervening two hundred yards of shoreline and reach Beatrice's apartment house. She met him as he stepped out of the elevator, wide-eyed with alarm.

'Robert, what's happening?' She put her hands on his shoulders and pressed her head against his damp shirt. 'Have you seen the alligators? There are thousands of them!'

'*Seen* them—I was damn' nearly eaten by one on your door-step.' Kerans released himself and hurried over to the window, pushed back the plastic vanes. The hydroplane had entered the central lagoon and was circling it at speed, the shoal of alligators following in its wake, those at the tail breaking off to station themselves at points around the shore. At least thirty or forty had remained in the lagoon below, and were cruising about slowly in small patrols, occasionally swerving on a careless iguana.

'Those devilish things must be their watch-guards,' Kerans decided. 'Like a tame troupe of tarantulas. Nothing better, when you come to think of it.'

Beatrice stood beside him, nervously fingering the collar of the jade silk shirt she wore over her black swim-suit. Although the apartment was beginning to look ramshackle and untidy, Beatrice continued to tend her own appearance devotedly. On the few occasions when Kerans called she would be sitting on the patio or before a mirror in her bedroom, automatically applying endless layers of patina, like a blind painter forever retouching a portrait he can barely remember for fear that otherwise he will forget it completely. Her hair was always dressed immaculately, the make-up on her mouth and eyes exquisitely applied, but her withdrawn, isolated gaze gave her the waxen, glacé beauty of an inanimate mannequin. At last, however, she had been roused.

'But who are they, Robert? That man in the speed-boat frightens me. I wish Colonel Riggs was here.'

'He'll be a thousand miles away by now, if he hasn't already reached Byrd. Don't worry, Bea. They may look a piratical crew, but there's nothing we can give them.'

A LARGE THREE-DECKER paddle-boat, paddles set fore and aft, had entered the lagoon, and was slowly moving over to the three scows drawn up a few yards from where Riggs' base had been moored. It was loaded with gear and cargo, decks crammed with large bales and canvas-swathed machinery, so that there was only six inches of freeboard amidships.

Kerans guessed that this was the group's depot ship, and that they were engaged, like most of the other freebooters still wandering through the Equatorial lagoons and archipelagos, in pillaging the drowned cities, reclaiming the heavy specialised machinery such as electrical power generators and switchgear that had been perforce abandoned by the governments. Nominally such looting was highly penalised, but in fact the authorities were only too eager to pay a generous price for any salvage.

'Look!'

Beatrice gripped Kerans' elbow. She pointed down at the testing station, where the rumpled, shaggy-haired figure of Dr. Bodkin stood on the roof, waving slowly at the men on the bridge of the paddle-boat. One of them, a bare-chested Negro in white slacks and a white peaked cap, began to shout back through a hailer.

Kerans shrugged. 'Alan's right. We've everything to gain by showing ourselves. If we help them they'll soon push off and leave us alone.'

Beatrice hesitated, but Kerans took her arm. The hydroplane, now free of its entourage, was crossing the central lagoon on its return, leaping lightly through the water on a beautiful wake of foam.

'Come on. If we get down to the jetty in time he'll probably give us a lift.'

8

THE MAN WITH
THE WHITE SMILE

HIS HANDSOME SATURNINE face regarding them with a mixture of suspicion and amused contempt, Strangman lounged back under the cool awning that shaded the poop deck of the depot ship. He had changed into a crisp white suit, the silk-like surface of which reflected the gilt plate of his high-backed Renaissance throne, presumably dredged from some Venetian or Florentine lagoon, and invested his strange personality with an almost magical aura.

'Your motives seem so complex, Doctor,' he remarked to Kerans. 'But perhaps you've given up hope of understanding them yourself. We shall label them the total beach syndrome and leave it at that.'

He snapped his fingers at the steward standing in the shadows behind him and selected an olive from the tray of small chow. Beatrice, Kerans and Bodkin sat in a semi-circle on the low couches, alternately chilled and roasted as the erratic air-conditioner above them varied its perimeter. Outside, half an hour before noon, the lagoon was a bowl of fire, the scattered light almost masking the tall apartment house on the opposite bank. The jungle was motionless in the immense heat, the alligators hiding in whatever shade they could find.

None the less, several of Strangman's men were messing about in one of the scows, unloading some heavy diving equipment under the direction of a huge hunchbacked Negro in a pair of green cotton shorts. A giant grotesque parody of a human being, now and then he took off his eye-patch to bellow abuse at them, and the mingled grunts and curses drifted across the steaming air.

'But tell me, Doctor,' Strangman pressed, apparently dissatisfied with Kerans' answers, 'when do you finally propose to leave?'

Kerans hesitated, wondering whether to invent a date. After waiting an hour for Strangman to change, he had offered their greetings to him and tried to explain why they were still there. However, Strangman seemed unable to take the explanation seriously, swinging abruptly from amusement at their naivety to sharp suspicion. Kerans watched him carefully, reluctant to make even the smallest false move. Whatever his real identity, Strangman was no ordinary freebooter. A curious air of menace pervaded the depot ship, its crew and their master. Strangman in particular, with his white smiling face, its cruel lines sharpening like arrows when he grinned, disturbed Kerans.

'We haven't really considered the possibility,' Kerans said. 'I think we all hope to stay on indefinitely. We have small stocks of supplies.'

'But, my dear man,' Strangman remonstrated, 'the temperature will soon be up to nearly two hundred degrees. The entire planet is rapidly returning to the Mesozoic Period.'

'Precisely,' Dr. Bodkin cut in, rousing himself for a moment from his introspection. 'And in so far as we are part of the planet, a piece of the main, we too are returning. This is our zone of transit, here we are re-assimilating our own biological pasts. That's why we have chosen to remain here. There is no ulterior motive, Strangman.'

'Of course not, Doctor. I completely respect your sincerity.' Shifts of mood seemed to cross and re-cross Strangman's face, making him look in turn irritable, amiable, bored and abstracted. He listened to an air-line pumping from the scow, then asked: 'Dr. Bodkin, did you live in London as a child? You must have many sentimental memories to recapture, of the great palaces and museums.' He added: 'Or are the only memories you have pre-uterine ones?'

Kerans looked up, surprised at the ease with which Strangman had mastered Bodkin's jargon. He noticed that Strangman was not only watching Bodkin shrewdly, but also waiting for any reaction from himself and Beatrice.

But Bodkin gestured vaguely. 'No, I'm afraid I remember nothing. The immediate past is of no interest to me.'

'What a pity,' Strangman rejoined archly. 'The trouble with you people is that you've been here for thirty million years and your perspectives are all wrong. You miss so much of the transitory beauty of life. I'm fascinated by the immediate past—the treasures of the Triassic compare pretty unfavourably with those of the closing years of the Second Millenium.'

He leaned around on one elbow and smiled at Beatrice, who sat with her hands discretely covering her bare knees, like a mouse observing a particularly fine cat. 'And what about you, Miss Dahl? You look a little melancholy. A touch of time-sickness, perhaps? The chronoclasmic bends?' He chuckled, amused by this sally, and Beatrice said quietly:

'We're usually rather tired here, Mr. Strangman. By the way, I don't like your alligators.'

'They won't hurt you.' Strangman leaned back and surveyed the trio. 'It's all very strange.' Over his shoulder he rapped a short command at the steward, then sat frowning to himself. Kerans realised that the skin of his face and hands was uncannily white, devoid altogether of any pigmentation. Kerans' heavy sunburn, like that of Beatrice and Dr. Bodkin, made him virtually indistinguishable from the remainder of the Negro crew, and the subtle distinctions between the mulattoes and quadroons had vanished. Strangman alone retained his original paleness, the effect emphasised by the white suit he had chosen.

The bare-chested Negro in the peaked cap appeared, sweat rilling across his powerful muscles. He was about six feet in height, but the rolling breadth of his shoulders made him seem stocky and compact. His manner was deferential and observant, and Kerans wondered how Strangman managed to maintain his authority over the crew, and why they accepted his harsh, callous tone.

Strangman introduced the Negro curtly. 'This is the Admiral, my chief whip. If I'm not around when you want me, deal with him.' He stood up, stepping down from the dais. 'Before you leave, let me take you on a brief tour of my treasure ship.' He extended an arm gallantly to Beatrice, who took it timorously, his eyes glinting and rapacious.

AT ONE TIME, Kerans surmised, the depot ship had been a gambling steamer and floating vice den, moored beyond the five-mile limit outside Messina or Beirut, or in the shelter of some estuarine creek under the blander, more tolerant skies south of the equator. As they left the deck a squad of men were lowering an ancient ornamental gangway to the water's edge, its banisters of peeling gilt shaded by a white clapboard marquee painted with gold tassels and drapery, creaking about on its pulleys like a funicular gazebo. The interior of the ship was decorated in a similar pastiche baroque. The bar, now dark and closed, at the forward end of the observation deck was like the stern castle of a ceremonial galleon, naked gilt caryatids supporting its portico. Semi-columns of fake marble formed little loggias that led away to the private alcoves and dining rooms, while the divided central stairway was a bad film set of Versailles, an aerial riot of dusty cupids and candelabra, the grimy brass overlayed with mould and verdigris.

But the former roulette wheels and chemin de fer tables had gone, and the scarred parquet flooring was covered with a mass of crates and cartons, piled up against the wire-mesh windows so that only a faint reflection of the light outside seeped through. Everything was well packed and sealed, but on an old mahogany chart table in one corner Kerans saw a collection of bronze and marble limbs and torsos, fragments of statuary waiting to be sorted.

Strangman paused at the bottom of the staircase, tearing off a strip of fading tempera from one of the murals. 'The place is falling to bits. Hardly up to the standard of the Ritz, Doctor. I envy your good sense.'

Kerans shrugged. 'It's a low-rent area now.' He waited as Strangman unlocked a door, and they entered the main storehold, a dim stifling cavern packed with large wooden crates, the floor strewn with sawdust. They were no longer in the refrigerated section of the ship, and the Admiral and another sailor followed them closely, continually hosing them with ice-cold air from a faucet on the wall. Strangman snapped his fingers and the Admiral quickly began to pull away the canvas wrappings draped between the crates.

In the thin light Kerans could just see the glimmering outline of a huge ornamented altarpiece at the far end of the hold, fitted with elaborate scroll-work and towering dolphin candelabra, topped by a neo-classical proscenium which would have covered a small house. Next to it stood a dozen pieces of statuary, mostly of the late Renaissance, stacks of heavy gilt frames propped against them. Beyond these were several smaller altarpieces and triptychs, an intact pulpit in panelled gold, three large equestrian statues, a few strands of sea-weed still entwined in the horses' manes, several pairs of enormous cathedral doors, embossed in gold and silver, and a large tiered marble fountain. The metal shelves around the side of the hold were loaded with smaller bric-à-brac: votive urns, goblets, shields and salvers, pieces of decorative armour, ceremonial inkstands and the like.

Still holding Beatrice's arm, Strangman gestured expansively a few yards ahead. Kerans heard him say 'Sistine Chapel' and 'Medici Tomb', but Bodkin muttered: 'Aesthetically, most of this is rubbish, picked for the gold content alone. Yet there's not much of that. What *is* the man up to?'

Kerans nodded, watching Strangman in his white suit, the bare-legged Beatrice beside him. Suddenly he remembered the Delvaux painting, with its tuxedoed skeletons. Strangman's chalk-white face was like a skull, and he had something of the skeletons' jauntiness. For no reason he began to feel an intense distaste for the man, his hostility more generalised than personal.

'Well, Kerans, what do you think of them?' Strangman pivoted at one end of the aisle and swung back, barking at the Admiral to cover the exhibits again. 'Impressed, Doctor?'

Kerans managed to take his eyes off Strangman's face and glanced at the looted relics.

'They're like bones,' he said flatly.

Baffled, Strangman shook his head. 'Bones? What on earth are you talking about? Kerans, you're insane! Bones, good God!'

As he let out a martyred groan, the Admiral took up the refrain, first saying the word quietly to himself as if examining a strange object, then repeating it more and more rapidly in a sort of nervous release, his broad face gibbering with laughter. The other sailor joined in, and together they began to chant it out, convulsed over the fire hose like snake dancers.

'Bones! Yes, man, dem's all bones! Dem bones dem bones dem . . . !'

Strangman watched them angrily, the muscles of his face locking and unlocking like manacles. Disgusted with this display of rudeness and bad temper, Kerans turned to leave the hold. In annoyance Strangman rushed after him, pressed the palm of his hand in Kerans' back and propelled him along the aisle out of the hold.

Five minutes later, as they drove off in one of the scows, the Admiral and half a dozen other members of the crew lined the rail, still chanting and dancing. Strangman had regained his humour, and stood coolly in his white suit, detached from the others, waving ironically.

9

THE POOL OF THANATOS

DURING THE NEXT two weeks, as the southern horizon became increasingly darkened by the approaching rain-clouds, Kerans saw Strangman frequently. Usually he would be driving his hydroplane at speed around the lagoons, his white lounge suit exchanged for overalls and helmet, supervising the work of the salvage teams. One scow, with six men, was working in each of the three lagoons, the divers methodically exploring the sunken buildings. Occasionally the placid routines of descent and pump would be interrupted by the sounds of rifle fire as an alligator venturing too near the divers was despatched.

Sitting in the darkness in his hotel suite, Kerans was far away from the lagoon, content to let Strangman dive for his loot as long as he would soon leave. More and more the dreams had begun to encroach on his waking life, his conscious mind becoming increasingly drained and withdrawn. The single plane of time on which Strangman and his men existed seemed so transparent as to have a negligible claim to reality. Now and then, when Strangman came to call on him, he would emerge for a few minutes on to this tenuous plane, but the real centre of his consciousness was elsewhere.

Curiously, after his initial irritation, Strangman had developed a sneaking liking for Kerans. The biologist's quiet, angular mind was a perfect target for Strangman's dry humour. At times he would subtly mimic Kerans, earnestly taking his arm during one of their dialogues and saying in a pious voice: 'You know, Kerans, leaving the sea two hundred million years ago may have been a deep trauma from which we've never recovered . . .'

On another occasion he sent two of his men over in a skiff to the lagoon; on one of the largest buildings on the opposite bank they painted in letters thirty feet high:

TIME ZONE

Kerans took this banter in good part, ignoring it when the divers' lack of success made it more acerbic. Sinking backwards through the past, he waited patiently for the coming of the rain.

It was after the diving party arranged by Strangman that Kerans first realised the true nature of his fear of the man.

Ostensibly the party had been devised by Strangman as a social function to bring the three exiles together. In his laconic, off-hand way Strangman had begun to lay siege to Beatrice, deliberately cultivating Kerans as a means of securing an easy entrée to her apartment. When he discovered that the members of the trio rarely saw each other he evidently decided on an alternative approach, bribing Kerans and Bodkin with the promise of his well-stocked cuisine and cellar. Beatrice, however, always refused these invitations to luncheon and midnight breakfast—Strangman and his entourage of alligators and one-eyed mulattoes still frightened her—and the parties were invariably cancelled.

But the real reason for his 'diving gala' was more practical. For some time he had noticed Bodkin punting around the creeks of the former university quarter—often the old man, much to his amusement, would be trailed around the narrow canals by one of the dragon-eyed scows, manned by the Admiral or Big Caesar and camouflaged with fern fronds, like a lost carnival float—

and attributing his own motives to others, assumed that Bodkin was searching for some long-buried treasure. The focus of his suspicions finally became fixed on the submerged planetarium, the one underwater building to which there was easy access. Strangman posted a permanent guard over the little lake, some two hundred yards to the south of the central lagoon, which contained the planetarium, but when Bodkin failed to appear at the dead of night in flippers and aqualung Strangman lost patience and decided to anticipate him.

'We'll pick you up at seven tomorrow morning,' he told Kerans. 'Champagne cocktails, cold buffet, we'll really find out what old Bodkin has got hidden down there.'

'I can tell you, Strangman. Just his lost memories. They're worth all the treasure in the world to him.'

But Strangman had let out a peal of sceptical laughter, roared away in the hydroplane and left Kerans hanging helplessly to the switchbacking jetty.

Promptly at seven the next morning the Admiral had come for him. They collected Beatrice and Doctor Bodkin and then repaired to the depot ship, where Strangman was completing his preparations for the dive. A second scow was filled with diving equipment—both aqualung and suit—pumps and a telephone. A diving cage hung from the davit, but Strangman assured them that the lake was free of iguanas and alligators and there was no need to remain in the cage underwater.

Kerans was sceptical of this, but for once Strangman was as good as his word. The lake had been cleared completely. Heavy steel grilles had been lowered into the water at the submerged entrances, and armed guards sat with harpoons and shot-guns astride the booms. As they entered the lake and moored against a shaded waterside balcony on the eastern side the last of a series of grenades was being tossed into the water, the sharp pulsing explosions spewing up a flotsam of stunned eels, shrimp and somasteroids, which were promptly raked away to one side.

The cauldron of submerged foam dispersed and cleared, and from their seats by the rail they looked down at the wide-domed roof of the planetarium, wreathed in strands of fucus, as Bodkin had said, like a giant shell-palace from a childhood fairy tale. The circular fanlight at the apex of the dome was covered by a retractable metal screen, and an attempt had been made to lift one of the sections, but to Strangman's chagrin they had long since rusted into place. The main entrance of the dome was at the original street level, too far down to be visible, but a preliminary reconnaissance had revealed that they would be able to enter without difficulty.

As the sunlight rose across the water Kerans gazed down into the green translucent depths, at the warm amnionic jelly through which he swam in his dreams. He remembered that despite its universal superabundance he had not fully immersed himself in the sea for ten years, and mentally recapitulated the motions of the slow breast-stroke that carried him through the water while he slept.

Three feet below the surface a small albino python swam past, searching for a way out of the enclosure. Watching its strong head swerve and dart as it evaded the harpoons, Kerans felt a momentary reluctance to entrust himself to the deep water. On the other side of the lake, behind one of the steel grilles, a large estuarine crocodile was wrestling with a group of sailors trying to drive it off. Big Caesar, his great legs clamped to the narrow sill of the boom, kicked savagely at the amphibian, which snapped and lunged at the spears and boat-hooks. Over thirty feet long, it was well over ninety years old, and measured six or seven feet in chest diameter. Its snow-white under-belly reminded Kerans that he had seen a curiously large number of albino snakes and lizards since Strangman's arrival, appearing from the jungle as if attracted by his presence. There had even been a few albino iguanas. One had sat on his jetty the previous morning, watching him like an alabaster lizard, and he had automatically assumed that it bore a message from Strangman.

Kerans looked up at Strangman, who stood in his white suit in the bows of the vessel, watching expectantly as the crocodile thrashed and slammed against the grille, almost toppling the giant Negro into the water. Strangman's sympathies were all too obviously with the crocodile, but not for any reasons of sportsmanship or from a sadistic desire to see one of his principal lieutenants gored and killed.

Finally, amid a confusion of shouts and curses, a shot-gun was passed to Big Caesar, who steadied himself and discharged both barrels into the hapless crocodile below his feet. With a bellow of pain, it backed away into the shallows, its tail smacking the water.

Beatrice and Kerans looked away, waiting for the coup de grâce to be administered, and Strangman swarmed along the rail in front of them, eager for a better vantage-point.

'When they're trapped or dying they smack the water as an alarm signal to each other.' He put a forefinger on Beatrice's cheek, as if trying to make her face the spectacle. 'Don't look so disgusted. Kerans! Damn it, show more sympathy for the beast. They've existed for a hundred million years; they're among the oldest creatures on the planet.'

After the animal had been dispatched he still stood elatedly by the rail, bouncing on the balls of his feet, as if hoping that it would resuscitate itself and make a come-back. Only when the decapitated head was hoisted away on the end of a boat-hook did he turn with a spasm of irritation to the business of the dive.

UNDER THE SUPERVISION of the Admiral, two of the crew made a preliminary dive in aqualungs. They climbed down the metal ladder into the water and glided away towards the sloping curve of the dome. They examined the fan-light, then tested the semicircular ribs of the building, pulling themselves across

the dome by the cracks in the surface. After their return a third
sailor descended, with suit and line. He clumped slowly across
the cloudy floor of the street below, the thin light reflected off
his helmet and shoulders. As the lines wound out, he entered the
main doorway and disappeared from view, communicating by
telephone with the Admiral, who sang out his commentary for
all to hear in a rich fruity baritone: 'In de pay-box . . . now in
de main lounge. . . . Jomo says de seats in de church, Captain
Strang', but de altar gone.'

Everyone was leaning over the rail, waiting for Jomo to reappear, but Strangman was slumped back moodily in his chair,
face clamped in one hand.

'Church!' he snorted derisively. 'God! Send someone else down.
Jomo's a bloody fool.'

'Yes, Captain.'

More divers descended, and the first champagne cocktails
were brought round by the steward. Intending to dive himself,
Kerans sipped lightly at the heady effervescence.

Beatrice touched his elbow, her face watchful. 'Are you going
down, Robert?'

Kerans smiled. 'To the basement, Bea. Don't worry. I'll use the
big suit; it's perfectly safe.'

'I wasn't thinking of that.' She looked up at the expanding
ellipse of the sun just visible over the roof-top behind them. The
olive-green light refracted through the heavy fern-fronds filled
the lake with a yellow, swampy miasma, drifting over the surface like vapour off a vat. A few moments earlier the water had
seemed cool and inviting, but now had become a closed world, the
barrier of the surface like a plane between two dimensions. The
diving cage was swung out and lowered into the water, its red
bars blurred and shimmering, so that the entire structure was
completely distorted. Even the men swimming below the surface
were transformed by the water, their bodies as they swerved and
pivoted turned into gleaming chimeras, like exploding pulses of
ideation in a neuronic jungle.

Far below them, the great dome of the planetarium hove out of the yellow light, reminding Kerans of some cosmic space vehicle marooned on Earth for millions of years and only now revealed by the sea. He leaned behind Beatrice and said to Bodkin: 'Alan, Strangman's searching for the treasure you've hidden down there.'

Bodkin smiled fleetingly. 'I hope he finds it,' he said mildly. 'The entire ransom of the Unconscious is waiting for him if he can.'

Strangman was standing in the bows of the craft, interrogating one of the divers who had surfaced and was now being helped out of his suit, water streaming off his copper skin across the deck. As he barked his questions he noticed Bodkin and Kerans whispering to each other. Brows knitting, he stalked across the deck to where they were sitting, watching them suspiciously through half-closed eyes, and then sidled behind them like a guard eyeing a trio of potentially troublesome prisoners.

Toasting him with his champagne cocktail, Kerans said jocularly: 'I was just asking Dr. Bodkin where he'd hidden his treasure, Strangman.'

Strangman paused, staring at him coldly as Beatrice laughed uneasily, hiding her face inside the wing collars of her beach shirt. He put his hands on the back of Kerans' wicker chair, his face like white flint. 'Don't worry, Kerans,' he snapped softly. 'I know where it is, and I don't need your help to find it.' He swung round on Bodkin. 'Do I, Doctor?'

Shielding one ear from the cutting edge of his voice, Bodkin murmured: 'I think you probably do know, Strangman.' He pushed his chair back into the shrinking shade. 'When does the gala begin?'

'Gala?' Strangman glanced about irritably, apparently forgetting that he had introduced the term himself. 'There are no bathing beauties here, Doctor; this isn't the local aquadrome. Wait a minute, though, I mustn't be ungallant and forget the beautiful Miss Dahl.' He bowed over her with an unctuous smile. 'Come, my dear, I'll make you queen of the aquacade, with an escort of fifty divine crocodiles.'

Beatrice looked away from his gleaming eyes. 'No, thanks, Strangman. The sea frightens me.'

'But you must. Kerans and Dr. Bodkin expect you to. And I. You'll be a Venus descending to the sea, made twice beautiful by your return.' He reached down to take her hand and Beatrice flinched from him, frowning with repugnance at his oleaginous smirk. Kerans pivoted in his seat and held her arm.

'I don't think this is Beatrice's day, Strangman. We only swim in the evenings, under a full moon. It's a question of mood, you know.'

He smiled at Strangman as the latter tightened his grip on Beatrice, his face like a white vampire's, as if becoming exasperated beyond all measure.

Kerans stood up. 'Look, Strangman, I'll take her place. All right? I'd like to go down and have a look at the planetarium.' He waved Beatrice's alarms aside. 'Don't worry, Strangman and the Admiral will take good care of me.'

'Of course, Kerans.' Strangman's good humour had returned, instantly he radiated a benevolent willingness to please, only the slightest hint in his eyes of his pleasure at having Kerans within his clutches. 'We'll put you in the big suit, then you can talk to us over the loudspeaker. Relax, Miss Dahl; there's no danger. Admiral! Suit for Dr. Kerans! Chop, chop!'

Kerans exchanged a brief warning glance with Bodkin, then looked away when he saw Bodkin's surprise at the alacrity with which he had volunteered. He felt curiously light-headed, though he had barely touched his cocktail.

'Don't go down for too long, Robert,' Bodkin called after him. 'The temperature of the water will be high, at least ninety-five degrees; you'll find it very enervating.'

Kerans nodded, then followed Strangman's eager stride to the forward deck. A couple of men were hosing down the suit and

helmet, while the Admiral and Big Caesar, and the sailors resting on the pump-wheels, watched Kerans approach with non-
committal interest.

'See if you can get down into the main auditorium,' Strangman
told him. 'One of the boys managed to find a slit in an exit door,
but the frame had rusted solid.' He examined Kerans with a
critical eye as he waited for the helmet to be lowered over his
head. Designed for use only within the first five fathoms, it was
a complete perspex bowl, braced by two lateral ribs, and afford-
ing maximum visibility. 'It suits you, Kerans, you look like the
man from inner space.' The rictus of a laugh twisted his face.
'But don't try to reach the Unconscious, Kerans; remember it isn't
equipped to go down that far!'

CLUMPING SLOWLY to the rail, the sailors carrying the lines
after him, Kerans paused to wave cumbersomely to Beatrice and
Dr. Bodkin, then mounted the narrow ladder and lowered himself slowly towards the slack green water below. It was shortly
after eight o'clock and the sun shone directly on to the tacky
vinyl envelope that enclosed him, clamming damply against his
chest and legs, and he looked forward with pleasure to cooling
his burning skin. The surface of the lake was now completely
opaque. A litter of leaves and weed floated slowly around it, occasionally disrupted by bubbles of trapped air erupting from the
interior of the dome.

To his right he could see Bodkin and Beatrice with their chins
on the rail, watching him expectantly. Directly above, on the
roof of the scow, stood the tall gaunt figure of Strangman, tails
of his jacket pushed back, arms akimbo, the light breeze lifting
his chalk-white hair. He was grinning soundlessly to himself,
but as Kerans' feet touched the water shouted something which
Kerans heard dimly relayed over the headphones. Immediately
the hiss of air through the intake valves in the helmet increased
and the internal circuit of the microphone came alive.

The water was hotter than he expected. Instead of a cool revivifying bath, he was stepping into a tank filled with warm, glutinous jelly that clamped itself to his calves and thighs like the foetid embrace of some gigantic protozoan monster. Quickly he lowered himself to his shoulders, then took his feet off the rungs and let his weight carry him slowly downwards into the green-lit deep, hand over hand along the the rail, and paused at the two-fathom mark.

Here the water was cooler, and he flexed his arms and legs thankfully, accustoming his eyes to the pale light. A few small angel fish swam past, their bodies gleaming like silver stars in the blue blur that extended from the surface to a depth of five feet, a 'sky' of light reflected from the millions of dust and pollen particles. Forty feet away from him loomed the pale curved hull of the planetarium, far larger and more mysterious than it had seemed from the surface, like the stern of an ancient sunken liner. The once polished aluminium roof had become dull and blunted, molluscs and bivalves clinging to the narrow ledges formed by the transverse vaulting. Lower down, where the dome rested on the square roof of the auditorium, a forest of giant fucus floated delicately from their pedestals, some of the fronds over ten feet tall, exquisite marine wraiths that fluttered together like the spirits of a sacred neptunian grove.

Twenty feet from the bottom the ladder ended, but Kerans was now almost at equilibrium with the water. He let himself sink downwards until he was holding the tips of the ladder above his head with his fingers, then released them and glided away backwards towards the lake floor, the twin antennae of his air-line and telephone cable winding up the narrow well of light reflected by the disturbed water to the silver rectangular hull of the scow.

Cut off by the water from any other sounds, the noise of the air pump and the relayed rhythms of his own respiration drummed steadily in his ears, increasing in volume as the air pressure was raised. The sounds seemed to boom around him in the dark olive-green water, thudding like the immense tidal pulse he had heard in his dreams.

A voice grated from his headphones: 'Strangman here, Kerans. How's the grey sweet mother of us all?'

'Feels like home. I've nearly reached the bottom now. The diving cage is over by the entrance.'

He sank to his knees in the soft loam which covered the floor, and steadied himself against a barnacled lamp-post. In a relaxed, graceful moon-stride he loped slowly through the deep sludge, which rose from his footprints like clouds of disturbed gas. On his right were the dim flanks of the buildings lining the sidewalk, the silt piled in soft dunes up to their first-floor windows. In the intervals between the buildings the slopes were almost twenty feet high, and the retaining grilles were locked into them like huge portcullises. Most of the windows were choked with debris, fragments of furniture and metal cabinets, sections of floorboards, matted together by the fucus and cephalopods.

The diving cage swung slowly on its cable five feet off the street, a selection of hacksaws and spanners loosely tied to the floor. Kerans approached the doorway of the planetarium, steering the lines behind him and occasionally pulled lightly off his feet when they became over-extended.

Like an immense submarine temple, the white bulk of the planetarium stood before him, illuminated by the vivid surface water. The steel barricades around the entrance had been dismantled by the previous divers, and the semicircular arc of doors which led into the foyer was open. Kerans switched on his helmet lamp and walked through the entrance. He peered carefully among the pillars and alcoves, following the steps which led up into the mezzanine. The metal railings and chromium display panels had rusted, but the whole interior of the planetarium, sealed off by the barricades from the plant and animal life of the lagoons, seemed completely untouched, as clean and untarnished as on the day the last dykes had collapsed.

Passing the ticket booth, he propelled himself slowly along the mezzanine, and paused by the rail to read the signs over the cloakroom doors, their luminous letters reflecting the light. A circular corridor led around the auditorium, the lamp throwing a pale cone of light down the solid black water. In the faint hope that the dykes would be repaired, the management of the planetarium had sealed a second inner ring of barricades around the auditorium, locked into place by padlocked cross-bars which had now rusted into immovable bulkheads.

The top right-hand corner panel of the second bulkhead had been jemmied back to provide a small peep-hole into the auditorium. Too tired by the water pressing on his chest and abdomen to lift the heavy suit, Kerans contented himself with a glimpse of a few motes of light gleaming through the cracks in the dome.

On his way to fetch a hacksaw from the diving cage, he noticed a small doorway at the top of a short flight of steps behind the ticket box, apparently leading over the auditorium, either a cineprojectionist's booth or the manager's office. He pulled himself up the handrail, the metal cleats of his weighted boots skating on the slimy carpet. The door was locked, but he drove his shoulders against it and the two hinges parted easily, the door gliding away gracefully across the floor like a paper sail.

Pausing to free his lines, Kerans listened to the steady pumping in his ears. The rhythm had changed perceptibly, indicating that a different pair of operators had taken over the job. They worked more slowly, presumably unaccustomed to pumping air at the maximum pressure. For some reason, Kerans felt a slight stirring of alarm. Although fully aware of Strangman's malice and unpredictability, he felt confident that he would not try to kill him by so crude a method as blocking the air supply. Both Beatrice and Bodkin were present, and although Riggs and his men were a thousand miles away there was always the chance that some specialist Government unit might pay a flying visit to the lagoons. Unless he killed Beatrice and Bodkin as well—which seemed unlikely, for a number of reasons (he obviously suspected them of knowing more about the city than they admitted)—Strangman would find Kerans' death more trouble than it was worth.

As the air hissed reassuringly through his helmet, Kerans moved forward across the empty room. A few shelves sagged from one wall, a filing cabinet loomed in a corner. Suddenly, with a shock of alarm, he saw what appeared to be a man in an immense ballooning space-suit facing him ten feet away, white bubbles streaming from his frog-like head, hands raised in an attitude of menace, a blaze of light pouring from his helmet. 'Strangman!' he shouted at it involuntarily.

'Kerans! What is it?' Strangman's voice, closer than the whisper of his own consciousness, cut across his panic. 'Kerans, you fool . . . !'

'Sorry, Strangman.' Kerans pulled himself together, and advanced slowly towards the approaching figure. 'I've just seen myself in a mirror. I'm up in the manager's office or control-room, I'm not sure which. There's a private stairway from the mezzanine, may be an entrance into the auditorium.'

'Good man. See if you can find the safe. It should be behind the picture frame directly over the desk.'

Ignoring him, Kerans placed his hands on the glass surface and swung the helmet sharply from left to right. He was in the control booth overlooking the auditorium, his image reflected in the glass sound-proof panel. In front of him was the cabinet which had once held the instrument console, but the unit had been removed, and the producer's swing-back seat faced out unobstructed like an insulated throne of some germ-obsessed potentate. Almost exhausted by the pressure of the water, Kerans sat down in the seat and looked out over the circular auditorium.

Dimly illuminated by the small helmet lamp, the dark vault with its blurred walls cloaked with silt rose up above him like a huge velvet-upholstered womb in a surrealist nightmare. The black opaque water seemed to hang in solid vertical curtains, screening the dais in the centre of the auditorium as if hiding the ultimate sanctum of its depths. For some reason the womb-like image of the chamber was reinforced rather than diminished by the circular rows of seats, and Kerans heard the thudding in his ears uncertain whether he was listening to the dim subliminal requiem of his dreams. He opened the small panel door which led down into the auditorium, disconnecting the telephone cable from his helmet so that he would be free of Strangman's voice.

A light coating of silt covered the carpeted steps of the aisle. In the centre of the dome the water was at least twenty degrees warmer than it had been in the control-room, heated by some freak of convection, and it bathed his skin like hot balm. The projector had been removed from the dais, but the cracks in the dome sparkled with distant points of light, like the galactic profiles of some distant universe. He gazed up at this unfamiliar zodiac, watching it emerge before his eyes like the first vision of some pelagic Cortez emerging from the oceanic deeps to glimpse the immense Pacifics of the open sky.

Standing on the dais, he looked around at the blank rows of seats facing him, wondering what uterine rite to perform for the invisible audience that seemed to watch him. The air pressure inside his helmet had increased sharply, as the men on the deck lost contact with him by telephone. The valves boomed off the sides of the helmet, the silver bubbles darted and swerved away from him like frantic phantoms.

Gradually, as the minutes passed, the preservation of this distant zodiac, perhaps the very configuration of constellations that had encompassed the Earth during the Triassic Period, seemed to Kerans a task more important than any other facing him. He stepped down from the dais and began to return to the control-room, dragging the air-line after him. As he reached the panel door he felt the line snake out through his hands, and with an impulse of anger seized a loop and anchored it around the handle of the door. He waited until the line tautened, then wound a second loop around the handle, providing himself with a radius of a dozen feet. He walked back down the steps and stopped half-way down the aisle, head held back, determined to engrave the image of the constellations on his retina. Already their patterns seemed more familiar than those of the classical constellations. In a vast, convulsive recession of the equinoxes, a billion sidereal days had reborn themselves, re-aligned the nebulae and island universes in their original perspectives.

A sharp spur of pain drove itself into his eustachian tube, forcing him to swallow. Abruptly he realised that the intake valve of the helmet supply was no longer working. A faint hiss seeped through every ten seconds, but the pressure had fallen steeply. Dizzying, he stumbled up the aisle and tried to free the airline from the handle, certain now that Strangman had seized the opportunity to fabricate an accident. Breath exploding, he tripped over one of the steps, fell awkwardly across the seats with a gentle ballooning motion.

As the spotlight flared across the domed ceiling, illuminating the huge vacant womb for the last time, Kerans felt the warm blood-filled nausea of the chamber flood in upon him. He lay back, spreadeagled across the steps, his hand pressed numbly against the loop of line around the door handle, the soothing pressure of the water penetrating his suit so that the barriers between his own private blood-stream and that of the giant amnion seemed no longer to exist. The deep cradle of silt carried him gently like an immense placenta, infinitely softer than any bed he had ever known. Far above him, as his consciousness faded, he could see the ancient nebulae and galaxies shining through the uterine night, but eventually even their light was dimmed and he was only aware of the faint glimmer of identity within the deepest recesses of his mind. Quietly he began to move towards it, floating slowly towards the centre of the dome,

knowing that this faint beacon was receding more rapidly than
he could approach it. When it was no longer visible he pressed
on through the darkness alone, like a blind fish in an endless forgotten sea, driven by an impulse whose identity he would never
comprehend. . . .

EPOCHS DRIFTED. Giant waves, infinitely slow and enveloping, broke and fell across the sunless beaches of the time-sea,
washing him helplessly in its shallows. He drifted from one pool
to another, in the limbos of eternity, a thousand images of himself reflected in the inverted mirrors of the surface. Within his
lungs an immense inland lake seemed to be bursting outwards,
his rib-cage distended like a whale's to contain the oceanic vol-
umes of water.

'KERANS. . . .'
   He looked up at the bright deck, at the brilliant panoply of
light on the canvas shade above him, at the watchful ebony face
of the Admiral sitting across his legs and pumping his chest in
his huge hands.
   'Strangman, he . . .' Choking on the expressed fluid in his
throat, Kerans let his head loll back on to the hot deck, the sunlight stinging his eyes. A circle of faces looked down at him
intently—Beatrice, her eyes wide with alarm, Bodkin frowning
seriously, a motley of brown faces under khaki képis. Abruptly a
single white grinning face interposed itself. Only a few feet from
him, it leered like an obscene statue.
   'Strangman, you—'
   The grin broke into a winning smile. 'No, I didn't, Kerans.
Don't try to pin the blame on me. Dr. Bodkin will vouch for
that.' He waggled a finger at Kerans. 'I warned you not to go
down too far.'
   The Admiral stood up, evidently satisfied that Kerans had
recovered. The deck seemed to be made of burning iron, and

Kerans pulled himself up on one elbow, sat weakly in the pool of water. A few feet away, creased in the scuppers, the suit lay like a deflated corpse.

Beatrice pushed through the circle of onlookers, and crouched down beside him. 'Robert, relax, don't think about it now.' She put her arm around his shoulders, glancing up watchfully at Strangman. He stood behind Kerans, grinning with pleasure, hands on hips.

'The cable seized . . .' Kerans cleared his head, his lungs like two bruised, tender flowers. He breathed slowly, soothing them with the cool air. 'They were pulling it from above. Didn't you stop . . .'

Bodkin stepped forward with Kerans' jacket and draped it across his shoulders. 'Easy, Robert; it doesn't matter now. Actually, I'm sure it wasn't Strangman's fault; he was talking to Beatrice and I when it happened. The cable was hooked round some obstruction, it looks as if it was a complete accident.'

'No, it wasn't, Doctor,' Strangman cut in. 'Don't perpetuate a myth, Kerans will be much more grateful for the truth. He anchored that cable himself, quite deliberately. Why?' Here Strangman tapped the air magisterially. 'Because he *wanted* to become part of the drowned world.' He began to laugh to himself, slapping his thighs with amusement as Kerans hobbled weakly to his chair. 'And the joke is that he doesn't know whether I'm telling the truth or not. Do you realise that, Bodkin? Look at him; he genuinely isn't sure! God, what irony!'

'Strangman!' Beatrice snapped at him angrily, overcoming her fears. 'Stop saying that! It might have been an accident.'

Strangman shrugged theatrically. 'It *might*,' he repeated with great emphasis. 'Let's admit that. It makes it more interesting— particularly for Kerans. *Did I or did I not try to kill myself?*' One of the few existential absolutes, far more significant than 'To be or not to be?', which merely underlines the uncertainty of the suicide, rather than the eternal ambivalence of his victim.' He smiled down patronisingly at Kerans as the latter sat quietly in his chair, sipping at the drink Beatrice had brought him. 'Kerans, I envy you the task of finding out—if you can.'

Kerans managed a weak smile. From the speed of his recovery he realised that he had suffered only mildly from the drowning. The remainder of the crew had moved away to their duties, no longer interested.

'Thank you, Strangman. I'll let you know when I have the answer.'

ON THE WAY BACK to the Ritz he sat silently in the stern of the scow, thinking to himself of the great womb-chamber of the planetarium and the multi-layered overlay of its associations, trying to erase from his mind the terrible 'either/or' which Strangman had correctly posed. Had he unconsciously locked the air-pipe, knowing that the tension in the cable would suffocate him, or had it been a complete accident, even, possibly, an attempt by Strangman to injure him? But for the rescue by the two skin divers (perhaps he had counted on them setting out after him when the telephone cable was disconnected) he would certainly have found the answer. His reasons for making the dive at all remained obscure. There was no doubt that he had been impelled by a curious urge to place himself at Strangman's mercy, almost as if he were staging his own murder.

During the next few days the conundrum remained unsolved. Was the drowned world itself, and the mysterious quest for the south which had possessed Hardman, no more than an impulse to suicide, an unconscious acceptance of the logic of his own devolutionary descent, the ultimate neuronic synthesis of the archaeopsychic zero? Rather than try to live with yet another enigma, and more and more frightened of the real role that Strangman played in his mind, Kerans systematically repressed his memories of the accident. Likewise, Bodkin and Beatrice ceased to refer to it, as if accepting that an answer to the question would solve for them many of the other mysterious enigmas which now alone sustained them, delusions which, like all the ambiguous but necessary assumptions about their own personalities, they would only sacrifice with reluctance.

10

SURPRISE PARTY

'KERANS . . . !'

Roused by the deep blare of the hydroplane as it approached the landing stage, Kerans stirred fretfully, his head lolling from side to side on the stale pillow. He focused his eyes on the bright green parallelogram which dappled the ceiling above the venetian blinds, listening to the engines outside reverse and accelerate, then with an effort pulled himself off the bed. It was already after 7.30, an hour later than he had woken a month earlier, and the brilliant sunlight reflected off the lagoon thrust its fingers into the darkened room like a ravenous golden monster.

With a pang of annoyance he noticed that he had forgotten to switch off the bedside fan before going to sleep. He had begun to fall asleep now at unpredictable moments, sometimes sitting half-upright on the bed while unlacing his shoes. In an attempt to conserve his fuel he had closed down the bedroom and moved the heavy gilt-framed double bed into the lounge, but its associations with sleep were so powerful that he was soon forced to move it back again.

'Kerans . . . !'

Strangman's voice echoed warningly down the corridor below.

Kerans limped slowly to the bathroom, managed to splash his face by the time Strangman let himself into the suite.

Tossing his helmet on to the floor, Strangman produced a decanter of hot black coffee and a canned gorgonzola green with age.

'A present for you.' He examined Kerans' dulled eyes with an amiable frown. 'Well, how are things in deep time?'

Kerans sat on the edge of the bed, waiting for the booming of the phantom jungles in his mind to fade. Like an endless shallows, the residues of the dreams stretched away below the surface of the reality around him. 'What brings you here?' he asked flatly.

Strangman put on an expression of deep injury.

'Kerans, I *like* you. You keep forgetting that.' He turned up the volume of the air-conditiner, smiling at Kerans, who gazed watchfully at the wry, perverted leer. 'Actually I have another motive— I want you to have dinner with me tonight. Don't start shaking your head. I have to keep coming here; it's time I returned your hospitality. Beatrice and old Bodkin will be there; it should be pretty swagger—fire-work displays, bongo drums *and* a surprise.'

'What exactly?'

'You'll see. Something really spectacular, believe me. I don't do things by halves. I'd have those 'gators dancing on the tips of their tails if I wanted to.' He nodded solemnly. 'Kerans, you're going to be impressed. And it may even do you some good mentally, stop this crazy time machine of yours.' His mood changed, becoming distant and abstracted. 'But I mustn't poke fun at you, Kerans, I couldn't bear a tenth of the personal responsibility you've shouldered. The tragic loneliness, for example, of those haunted Triassic swamps.' He picked a book off the air-conditioner, a copy of Donne's poems, and extemporised a line: 'World within world, each man an island unto himself, swimming through seas of archipelagos. . . .'

Fairly certain that he was fooling, Kerans asked: 'How's the diving going?'

'Frankly, not very well. The city's too far north for much to have been left. But we've discovered a few interesting things. You'll see tonight.'

Kerans hesitated, doubting whether he would have enough energy to make small talk with Dr. Bodkin and Beatrice—he had seen neither of them since the debacle of the diving party, though every evening Strangman drove over in his hydroplane to Beatrice's apartment house (what success he had Kerans could only guess, but Strangman's references to her—'Women are like spiders, they sit there watching you and knitting their webs' or 'She keeps talking about *you*, Robert, confound her'—indicated a negative response.)

However, the particular twist of emphasis in Strangman's voice suggested that Kerans' attendance was obligatory, and that he would not be allowed to refuse. Strangman followed him into the lounge, waiting for a reply.

'It's rather short notice, Strangman.'

'I'm terribly sorry, Kerans, but as we know each other so well I felt sure you wouldn't mind. Blame it on my manic-depressive personality. I'm always seizing on wild schemes.'

Kerans found two gold-plated porcelain coffee cups and filled them from the decanter. Know each other so well, he repeated to himself ironically. I'm damned if I know you at all, Strangman. Racing around the lagoons like the delinquent spirit of the drowned city, apotheosis of all its aimless violence and cruelty, Strangman was half-buccaneer, half-devil. Yet he had a further neuronic role, in which he seemed almost a positive influence, holding a warning mirror up to Kerans and obliquely cautioning him about the future he had chosen. It was this bond that kept them together, for otherwise Kerans would long since have left the lagoons and moved southwards.

'I assume this isn't a farewell celebration?' he asked Strangman. 'You aren't leaving us?'

'Kerans, of course not,' Strangman remonstrated. 'We've only just got here. Besides,' he added sagely, 'where would we go? There's nothing much left now—I can tell you, I sometimes feel like Phlebas the Phoenician. Though that's really your role, isn't it?

> A current under sea
> Picked his bones in whispers. As he rose and fell
> He passed the stages of his age and youth
> Entering the whirlpool.'

He continued to pester Kerans until the latter accepted his invitation, then made off jubilantly. Kerans finished the coffee in the decanter, when he began to recover drew the venetian blinds and let in the bright sunlight.

Outside, in his chair on the veranda, a white monitor lizard sat and regarded him with its stony eyes, waiting for something to happen.

AS HE RODE across the lagoon to the paddle-ship that evening, Kerans speculated on the probable nature of Strangman's 'surprise', hoping that it would not be some elaborate practical joke. The effort of shaving off his beard and putting on a white dinner jacket had tired him.

Considerable preparations were obviously afoot in the lagoon. The depot ship had been moored about fifty yards from shore, strung with awnings and coloured lights, and the two remaining scows were working systematically along the banks, driving the alligators into the central lagoon.

Kerans pointed to a big caiman thrashing about in a circle of boat-hooks, and said to Big Caesar: 'What's on the menu tonight—roast alligator?'

The giant hunch-backed mulatto at the helm of the scow shrugged with studied vagueness. 'Strang' got a big show tonight, Mistah Kerans, a real big show. You see.'

Kerans left his seat and leaned on the bridge. 'Big Caesar, how long have you known the Captain?'

'Long time, Mistah Kerans. Ten years, maybe twenty.'

'He's a strange one, all right,' Kerans continued. 'His moods change so quickly—you must have noticed that, working for him. Sometimes he frightens me.'

The big mulatto smiled cryptically. 'You right there, Mistah Kerans,' he rejoined with a chuckle. 'You really right.'

But before Kerans could press him a megaphone jabbed at them across the water from the bridge of the depot ship.

STRANGMAN MET each one of his guests as they arrived at the head of the gangway. In high spirits, he managed a sustained mood of charm and good cheer, complimenting Beatrice elaborately on her appearance. She wore a full-length blue brocade ball dress, the turquoise mascara around her eyes making her look like some exotic bird of paradise. Even Bodkin had contrived to trim his beard and salvage a respectable linen jacket, an old piece of crepe around his neck a ragged concession to a black tie. Like Kerans, however, they both seemed glazed and remote, joining in the conversation over dinner automatically.

Strangman, however, failed to notice this, or if he did was too elated and preoccupied to care. Whatever his motives, he had obviously gone to considerable trouble to stage his surprise. A fresh canvas awning had been broken out like a crisp white sail over the observation deck, flared at its rim in the form of an inverted marquee to give them an uninterrupted view over the lagoon and sky. A large circular dining table stood by the rail, low divans in the Egyptian style, with spiral gilt and ivory bolsters, disposed around it. A clutter of unmatched but none the less brilliant pieces of gold and silver dining plate decorated the table, much of it of huge proportions—the ormolu finger-bowls were the size of face baths.

Strangman had rifled his treasure house below in an access

of profligacy—several pieces of blackened bronze statuary stood about behind the table bearing salvers of fruit and orchids, and an immense canvas by some painter of the school of Tintoretto had been propped against the funnels and screened the service hatches, looming down over the table like a mural. Its title was 'The Marriage of Ester and King Xerxes', but the pagan treatment and the local background of the Venetian lagoon and the Grand Canal palazzos, coupled with the Quinquecento décor and costume, made it seem more like 'The Marriage of Neptune and Minerva', no doubt the moral Strangman intended to point. King Xerxes, a wily, beak-nosed elderly Doge or Venetian Grand-Admiral, already seemed completely tamed by his demure, raven-haired Ester, who had a faint but none the less perceptible likeness to Beatrice. As he cast his eye over the crowded spread of the canvas with its hundreds of wedding guests, Kerans suddenly saw another familiar profile—the face of Strangman among the hard cruel smiles of the Council of Ten—but when he approached the painting the similarity vanished.

The marriage ceremony was being celebrated aboard a galleon moored against the Doge's Palace, and its elaborate rococo rigging seemed to merge directly into the steel hawsers and bracing lines of the depot ship. Apart from the kindred settings, emphasised by the two lagoons and the buildings rising from the water, Strangman's motley crew might themselves have stepped straight from the canvas, with its jewelled slaves and Negro captain of gondoliers.

Sipping his cocktail, Kerans said to Beatrice: 'Do you see yourself there, Bea? Obviously, Strangman hopes you'll subdue the flood-waters with the same skill Ester used to pacify the King.'

'Correct, Kerans!' Strangman stepped over to them from the bridge. 'You have it exactly.' He bowed to Beatrice. 'I hope you accept the compliment, my dear?'

'I'm very flattered, Strangman, of course.' Beatrice moved over to the painting, examining her double, then turned in a swirl of brocade and stood by the rail, staring out over the water. 'But I'm not sure whether I want to be cast in that role, Strangman.'

'But you are, Miss Dahl, inescapably.' Strangman gestured the steward over to Bodkin, who was sitting in a quiet reverie, then slapped Kerans on the shoulder. 'Believe me, Doctor, you'll soon see—'

'Good. I'm getting a little impatient, Strangman.'

'What, after thirty million years you can't wait five minutes? I'm obviously bringing you back to the present.'

Throughout the meal Strangman supervised the succession of wines, taking advantage of his absences from the table to confer with the Admiral. With the final brandies before them, Strangman sat down apparently for the last time, winking broadly at Kerans. Two of the scows had moved over to the inlet by the far side of the lagoon and disappeared into its mouth, while the third took up its position in the centre, from where it released a small firework display.

The last sunlight still lay over the water, but had faded sufficiently for the bright catherine wheels and rockets to flicker and dazzle, their sharp explosions etched clearly against the tinted crepuscular sky. The smile on Strangman's face grew broader and broader, until he lay back on his chesterfield grinning soundlessly to himself, the red and green flashes illuminating his saturnine features.

Uncomfortably, Kerans leaned forward to ask him when their surprise would materialise, but Strangman anticipated him.

'Well, haven't you noticed?' He glanced around the table. 'Beatrice? Dr. Bodkin? You three are slow. Come out of deep time for a moment.'

A curious silence hung over the ship, and involuntarily Kerans leaned against the rail to brace himself in case Strangman was about to set off an underwater explosive charge. Glancing down at the deck below, he suddenly saw the twenty or thirty members of the crew, looking motionlessly at the lagoon, their ebony faces

and white singlets flickering with the ghostly light, like the crew
of a spectral ship.

Puzzled, Kerans searched the sky and lagoon. The dusk had
come in rather more quickly than he expected, the curtain walls
of the buildings opposite sinking into shadow. At the same time
the sky remained clear and visible in the sunset, the tops of the
surrounding vegetation brilliantly tinted.

A low drumming sounded somewhere in the distance, the
air-pumps which had worked all day and whose noise had been
masked by the pyrotechnic display. Around the ship the water
had become strangely slack and lifeless, the low swells that usually disturbed it absent. Wondering whether an exhibition of
underwater swimming had been arranged for a troupe of trained
alligators, he peered down at the surface.

'Alan! Look, for heaven's sake! Beatrice, can you see?' Kerans
kicked back his chair and leapt to the rail, pointing down in
amazement at the water. 'The level is going down!'

Looming just below the dark pellucid surface were the dim
rectangular outlines of the submerged buildings, their open windows like empty eyes in enormous drowned skulls. Only a few
feet from the surface, they drew closer, emerging from the depths
like an immense intact Atlantis. First a dozen, then a score of
buildings appeared to view, their cornices and fire escapes clearly
visible through the thinning refracting glass of the water. Most
of them were only four or five storeys high, part of a district of
small shops and offices enclosed by the taller buildings that had
formed the perimeter of the lagoon.

Fifty yards away the first of the roofs broke surface, a blunted
rectangle smothered with weeds and algae, across which slith-
ered a few desperate fish. Immediately half a dozen others
appeared around it, already roughly delineating a narrow street.
The upper line of windows emerged, water spilling from their
ledges, fucus draped from the straggling wires that sagged across
the roadways.

Already the lagoon had vanished. As they sank slowly downwards, settling into what seemed to be a large open square, they were now looking across a diffuse straggle of roof-tops, punctuated by eroded chimneys and spires, the flat sheet of the surface transformed into a jungle of cubist blocks, at its boundaries merging into the higher ground of the enveloping vegetation. What remained of the water had formed into distinct channels, dark and sombre, eddying away around corners and into narrow alleyways.

'Robert! Stop it! It's horrible!' Kerans felt Beatrice seize his arm, her long blue nails biting through the fabric of his dinner jacket. She gazed out at the emerging city, an expression of revulsion on her tense face, physically repelled by the sharp acrid smells of the exposed water-weeds and algae, the damp barnacled forms of rusting litter. Veils of scum draped from the criss-crossing telegraph wires and tilting neon signs, and a thin coating of silt cloaked the faces of the buildings, turning the once limpid beauty of the underwater city into a drained and festering sewer.

For a moment Kerans fought to free his mind, grappling with this total inversion of his normal world, unable to accept the logic of the rebirth before him. First he wondered whether there had been a total climatic reversal that was shrinking the formerly expanding seas, draining the submerged cities. If so, he would have to make his way back to this new present, or be marooned millions of years away on the beach of some lost Triassic lagoon. But deep within his mind the great sun pounded dimly with a strength still undiminished, and beside him he heard Bodkin mutter:

'Those pumps are powerful. The water is going down by a good two or three feet a minute. We're not far from the bottom now. The whole thing's fantastic!'

Laughter rocked out into the darkening air as Strangman rolled about mirthfully on the chesterfield, dabbing his eyes with a napkin. Released from the tension of staging the spectacle, he was now exulting in the three bewildered faces at the rail. On the bridge above him, the Admiral watched with dry amusement, the fading light glinting across his bare chest like a gong. Two or three men below were taking in the mooring lines, holding the orientation of the ship in the square.

The two scows which had moved over to the creek mouth during the firework display were floating behind a massive boom, and a foaming mass of water poured from the twin vents of a huge pumping system. Then the rooftops obscured their view across the interval, and the people on the deck were looking up at the blanched buildings of the square. Only fifteen or twenty feet of water remained, and a hundred yards away down one of the side streets they could see the third scow wending tentatively below the trailing wires.

Strangman controlled himself and came over to the rail. 'Perfect, don't you agree, Dr. Bodkin? What a jest, a really superb spectacle! Come on, Doctor, don't look so piqued. Congratulate me! It wasn't too easy to arrange.'

Bodkin nodded and moved away along the rail, his face still stunned. Kerans asked: 'But how did you seal off the perimeter? There's no continuous wall around the lagoon.'

'There is now, Doctor. I thought you were the expert in marine biology. The fungi growing in the swamp mud outside consolidated the entire mass; for the last week there's only been one point of influx; took us five minutes to dam it up.'

He gazed out brightly at the emerging streets in the dim light around them, the humped backs of cars and buses appearing through the surface. Giant anemones and star-fish flopped limply in the shallows, collapsing kelp straggled out of windows.

Numbly, Bodkin said: 'Leicester Square.'

His laughter vanishing, Strangman swung on him, his eyes peering rapaciously at the neon-covered porticos of the hulks of former cinemas and theatres.

'So you *do* know your way around here, Doctor! A pity you

couldn't have helped us before, when we were getting nowhere.' He slammed the rail with an oath, jarring Kerans' elbow. 'By God, though, we're really in business now!' With a snarl he flung himself away from them, kicking back the dining table, shouting up at the Admiral.

BEATRICE WATCHED HIM disappear below with alarm, a slender hand on her throat. 'Robert, he's insane. What are we going to do?—He'll drain all the lagoons.'

Kerans nodded, thinking about the transformation of Strangman which he had witnessed. With the reappearance of the submerged streets and buildings his entire manner had changed abruptly. All traces of courtly refinement and laconic humour had vanished; he was now callous and vulpine, the renegade spirit of the hoodlum streets returning to his lost playground. It was almost as if the presence of the water had anaesthetised him, smothering his true character so that only the surface veneer of charm and moodiness remained.

Behind them the shadow of an office block fell across the deck, drawing a diagonal curtain of darkness over the huge painting. A few figures, Ester and the Negro captain of gondoliers, still remained, and a single white face, a beardless member of the Council of Ten. As Strangman had prophesied, Beatrice had performed her symbolic role, Neptune had deferred and withdrawn.

Kerans looked up at the round bulk of the testing station, poised on the cinema behind them like an enormous boulder on the edge of a cliff. Apparently eighty to ninety feet higher, the tall buildings around the lagoon perimeter now cut off half the sky, enclosing them in dim canyon floor world.

'It doesn't matter that much,' Kerans temporised. He steadied her against his arm as the ship touched bottom and rolled slightly, crushing a small car under the port bow. 'When he's finished stripping the stores and museums they'll leave. Anyway, the rain-storms will be here in a week or two.'

Beatrice cleared her throat distastefully, wincing as the first bats flickered among the roof-tops, darting from one dripping eave to another. 'But it's all so hideous. I can't believe that anyone ever lived here. It's like some imaginary city of Hell. Robert, I *need* the lagoon.'

'Well, we could leave and move south across the silt flats. What do you think, Alan?'

Bodkin shook his head slowly, still staring out blankly at the darkened buildings around the square. 'You two go, I must stay here.'

Kerans hesitated. 'Alan,' he warned him gently. 'Strangman has everything he needs now. We're useless to him. Soon we'll simply be unwelcome guests.'

But Bodkin ignored him. He looked down at the streets, hands clasping the rail like an old man at the counter of some vast store, shopping for the memories of his childhood.

The streets had almost been drained. The approaching scow ran aground on the sidewalk, pushed off again and then stuck finally on a traffic island. Led by Big Caesar, the three-man crew jumped down into the waist-deep water and waded noisily towards the depot ship, splashing water excitedly into the open shop-fronts.

With a jolt the paddle-ship settled itself firmly on the bottom, cheers and shouts going up from Strangman and the rest of the crew as they fended off the snapping overhead wires and tilted telegraph poles. A small dinghy was thrown into the water, and to a chorus of fists pounding a drum-beat on the rail the Admiral rowed Strangman across the shallow pool to the fountain in the centre of the square. Here Strangman debarked, pulled a flare pistol from a pocket of his dinner jacket and with an exultant shout began to fire salvo after salvo of coloured star-shells into the air overhead.

11

'THE BALLAD OF
MISTAH BONES'

HALF AN HOUR later Beatrice, Kerans and Dr. Bodkin were able to walk out into the streets. Huge pools of water still lay about everywhere, leaking from the ground floors of the buildings, but they were little more than two or three feet deep. There were clear stretches of pavement over a hundred yards long, and many of the further streets were completely drained. Dying fish and marine plants expired in the centre of the roadways, and huge banks of black sludge were silted up into the gutters and over the sidewalks, but fortunately the escaping waters had cut long pathways through them.

Strangman at their head, racing along in his white suit, firing star-shells into the dark streets, the crew charged off in a bellowing pack, those in front balancing a rum keg on their upturned palms, the others brandishing an assortment of bottles, machetes and guitars. A few derisive shouts of 'Mistah Bones!' faded around Kerans as he helped Beatrice down off the gangway, and then the trio were left alone in the silence of the huge stranded paddle-ship.

Glancing up uncertainly at the high distant ring of the jungle looming out of the darkness like the encircling lip of an extinct volcanic cone, Kerans led the way across the pavement to the nearest buildings. They stood in the entrance to one of the huge cinemas, sea urchins and cucumbers flickering faintly across the tiled floor, sand dollars flowering in the former ticket booth.

Beatrice gathered her skirt in one hand, and they moved slowly down the line of cinemas, past cafés and amusement arcades, patronised now only by the bivalves and molluscs. At the first corner they turned away from the sounds of revelry coming from the other side of the square, and walked westwards down the dim dripping canyons. A few star-shells continued to explode overhead, and the delicate glass sponges in the doorways glowed softly as they reflected the pink and blue light.

'Coventry Street, Haymarket . . .' Kerans read off the rusting street signs. They stepped quickly into a doorway as Strangman and his pack charged back across the square in a blaze of light and noise, machetes slashing at the rotting boards over the shop-fronts.

'Let's hope they find something that satisfies them,' Bodkin murmured. He searched the crowded skyline, as if looking for the deep black water that had once covered the buildings.

For several hours they wandered like forlorn elegant ghosts through the narrow streets, occasionally meeting one of the roistering crew, ambling drunkenly along the centre of the roadway with the remains of some fading garment in one hand, a machete in the other. A few small fires had been started in the centre of the street junctions, groups of two or three men warming themselves over the flaring tinder.

Avoiding these, the trio made their way across the nexus of streets to the south shore of the sometime lagoon, where Beatrice's apartment house rose up into the darkness, the penthouse lost among the stars.

'You'll have to walk the first ten storeys,' Kerans told Beatrice. He pointed to the deep bank of silt which reached upwards in a damp concave slope to the fifth floor windows, part of an immense massif of coagulated loam which, as Strangman had described, now encircled the lagoon and formed an impenetrable dyke against the encroaching sea. Down the side-streets they could see the great viscous mass lifting over the roof-tops, flowing through the gutted buildings, which in turn helped to rigidify them.

Here and there the perimeter of the dyke moored itself to a heavier obstruction—a church or government office—and diverged from its circular path around the lagoon. One of these evaginations followed the route they had taken on their way to the diving party, and Kerans felt his step quicken as they approached the planetarium. He waited impatiently as the others idled in front of the empty display windows of the old department stores, or gazed at the black slime oozing down the escalators below the office blocks into sluggish pools across the street.

Even the smallest of the buildings had been barricaded before being abandoned, and a makeshift clutter of steel screens and grilles collapsed across the doorways, hiding whatever might lie behind them. Everything was covered with a fine coating of silt, smothering whatever grace and character had once distinguished the streets, so that the entire city seemed to Kerans to have been resurrected from its own sewers. Were the Day of Judgement to come, the armies of the dead would probably rise clothed in the same filthy mantle.

'Robert.' Bodkin held his arm, pointing down the darkened street ahead of them. Fifty yards away, its metal dome outlined faintly in the fragmentary light of the distant signal rockets, stood the sombre, shadow-draped hull of the planetarium. Kerans stopped, recognising the orientation of the surrounding roadway, the sidewalks and street lamps, then walked forward, half uncertain, half curious, towards this pantheon which held so many of his terrors and enigmas.

Sponges and red kelp sagged limply across the sidewalk outside the entrance as they approached, picking their way carefully over the banks of mud that lined the street. The groves of wraith-like fucus which had wreathed the dome now flopped limply over the portico, their long draining fronds hanging over the entrance like a ragged awning. Kerans reached up and pushed aside the fronds, then peered cautiously into the interior of the darkened foyer. Thick black mud, hissing faintly as its contained marine life expired in a slow deflation of air-bladders and buoyancy sacs, lay everywhere, over the ticket booths and the stairway to the mezzanine, across the walls and door-panels. No longer the velvet mantle he remembered from his descent, it was now a fragmenting cloak of rotting organic forms, like the vestments of the grave. The once translucent threshold of the womb had vanished, its place taken by the gateway to a sewer.

Kerans began to walk forwards across the foyer, remembering the deep twilight bower of the auditorium and its strange zodiac. Then he felt the dark fluid rilling out across the mud between his feet, like the leaking blood-stream of a whale.

Quickly he took Beatrice's arm, and retraced their steps down the street. 'I'm afraid the magic has gone,' he re-remarked flatly. He forced a laugh. 'I suppose Strangman would say that the suicide should never return to the scene of his crime.'

ATTEMPTING TO TAKE a shorter route, they blundered into a winding cul-de-sac, managed to step back in time as a small caiman lunged at them from a shallow pool. Darting between the rusting shells of cars, they regained the open street, the alligator racing behind them. It paused by a lamp post on the edge of the sidewalk, tail whipping slowly, jaws flexing, and Kerans pulled Beatrice after him. They broke into a run and had covered ten yards when Bodkin slipped and fell heavily into a bank of silt.

'Alan! Hurry!' Kerans started to go back for him, the caiman's head pivoting towards them. Marooned behind in the lagoon, it seemed bewildered and ready to attack anything.

Suddenly there was a roar of gunfire, the flames stabbing across the roadway. Flares held above their heads, a group of men appeared around a corner. In front of them was the white-faced figure of Strangman, followed by the Admiral and Big Caesar, shot-guns at their shoulders.

Strangman's eyes glittered in the flare light. He made a small bow towards Beatrice, then saluted Kerans. Its spine shattered, the alligator thrashed impotently in the gutter, revealing its yellow underbelly, and Big Caesar drew his machete and began to hack at its head.

Strangman watched it with evil pleasure. 'Loathsome brute,' he commented, then pulled from his pocket a huge rhinestone necklace, still encrusted with algae, and held it out to Beatrice.

'For you, my dear.' Deftly, he strung the strands around her neck, regarding the effect with pleasure. The entwined weeds among the sparkling stones against the white skin of her breast made her look like some naiad of the deep. 'And all the other jewels of this dead sea.'

With a flourish he was off again, the flares vanishing in the darkness with the shouts of his men, leaving them alone in the silence with the white jewels and the decapitated alligator.

DURING THE NEXT DAYS events proceeded to even greater madness. Increasingly disorientated, Kerans would wander alone through the dark streets at night—by day it became unbearably hot in the labyrinth of alleyways—unable to tear himself away from his memories of the old lagoon, yet at the same time locked fast to the empty streets and gutted buildings.

After his first surprise at seeing the drained lagoon he began to sink rapidly into a state of dulled inertia, from which he tried helplessly to rouse himself. Dimly he realised that the lagoon had represented a complex of neuronic needs that were impossible to satisfy by any other means. This blunting lethargy deepened, unbroken by the violence around him, and more and more he felt like a man marooned in a time sea, hemmed in by the shifting planes of dissonant realities millions of years apart.

The great sun beating in his mind almost drowned out the sounds of the looting and revelry, the roars of explosives and shot-guns. Like a blind man he stumbled in and out of the old arcades and entrances, his white dinner suit stained and grimy, jeered at by the sailors as they charged by him, playfully buffeting his shoulders. At midnight he would wander feverishly through the roistering singers in the square and sit beside Strangman at his parties, hiding back under the shadow of the paddle-ship, watching the dancing and listening to the beat of the drums and guitars, overlayed in his mind by the insistent pounding of the black sun.

He abandoned any attempt to return to the hotel—the creek was blocked by the pumping scows, and the intervening lagoon seethed with alligators—and during the day either slept in Beatrice's apartment on the sofa or sat numbly in a quiet alcove on the gaming deck of the depot ship. Most of the crew would be asleep among the crates or arguing over their spoils, waiting with surly impatience for the dusk, and they left him alone. By an inversion of logic it was safer to stay close to Strangman than to try to continue his previous separate regimen. Bodkin attempted this, withdrawing in a growing state of shock to the testing station—now reached by a precipitous climb up a dilapidated fire escape—but on one of his midnight forays out into the streets of the university quarter behind the planetarium he had been seized by a group of sailors and roughly manhandled. By attaching himself to Strangman's entourage Kerans had at least conceded his absolute authority over the lagoons.

Once he managed to force himself to visit Bodkin, found him resting quietly in his bunk, cooled by a home-made fan and the fading air-conditioner. Like himself, Bodkin seemed to be isolated on a small spur of reality in the centre of the time sea.

'Robert,' he murmured through his swollen lips, 'get away from here. Take her, the girl'—here he searched for the name—'Beatrice, and find another lagoon.'

Kerans nodded, hunching himself inside the narrow cone of cool air projected by the air-conditioner. 'I know, Alan, Strangman's insane and dangerous, but for some reason I can't leave yet. I don't know why, but there's something here—those naked streets.' He gave up cloudily. 'What is it? There's a strange incubus on my mind. I must lift it first.'

Bodkin managed to sit up weakly. 'Kerans, listen. Take her and go. Tonight. Time doesn't exist here now.'

In the laboratory below, a pallid brown scum was draped over the great semicircle of progress charts, Bodkin's dismembered neuronic zodiac, and veiled the stranded benches and fume cupboards. Kerans made a half-hearted attempt to replace the charts that had fallen to the floor, then gave up and spent the next hour washing his silk dinner jacket in a pool of water left behind in one of the sinks.

Perhaps in imitation of himself, several of the crew now also sported tuxedos and black ties. A pantechnicon full of evening wear sealed inside watertight tin envelopes had been found in one of the warehouses. Egged on by Strangman, half a dozen of the sailors dressed themselves up, bow ties around their bare necks, and pranced through the streets in tremendous glee, tails flaring and knees high-kicking, like a troupe of lunatic waiters at a dervish carnival.

After the initial abandon, the looting began to take on a more serious note. Whatever his private reasons, Strangman was solely interested in objets d'art, and after a careful reconnaissance identified one of the city's principal museums. But, to his annoyance, the building had been stripped, and his only salvage was a large mosaic which his men removed tile by tile from the entrance hall and laid out like a vast jig-saw on the observation deck of the depot ship.

This disappointment prompted Kerans to warn Bodkin that Strangman might try to vent his spleen on him, but when he climbed up to the testing station early the next evening he found that Bodkin had gone. The air-conditioner had exhausted its fuel, and Bodkin, deliberately it seemed, had opened the windows before he left, so that the entire station steamed like a cauldron.

Curiously, Bodkin's disappearance gave Kerans little concern. Immersed in himself, he merely assumed that the biologist had followed his own advice and moved out to one of the lagoons to the south.

Beatrice, however, was still there. Like Kerans, she had sunk into a private reverie. Kerans rarely saw her during the day, when she would be locked into her bedroom, but at midnight, when it became cool, she would always come down from her penthouse among the stars and join Strangman at his parties. She sat numbly beside him in her blue evening dress, her hair studded with three or four of the tiaras Strangman had looted from the old jewellery vaults, her breasts smothered under a mass of glittering chains and crescents, like a mad queen in a horror drama.

Strangman treated her with a strange deference, not unmarked by a polite hostility, almost as if she were a tribal totem, a deity whose power was responsible for their continued good fortune but none the less resented. Kerans tried to stay near her, within her orbit of protection, and the evening after Bodkin's disappearance leaned across the cushions to say: 'Alan's gone. Old Bodkin. Did he see you before he left?'

But Beatrice stared out over the fires burning in the square, without looking at him said in a vague voice: 'Listen to the drumming, Robert. How many suns are there, do you think?'

WILDER NOW THAN Kerans had ever seen him, Strangman danced about the camp-fires, sometimes forcing Kerans to join him, inciting the bongo drummers to ever faster rhythms. Then, exhausted, he would slump back on his divan, his thin white face like blue chalk.

Leaning on one elbow, he stared sombrely at Kerans, squatting on a cushion behind him.

'Do you know why they fear me, Kerans? The Admiral, Big
Caesar and the others. Let me tell you my secret.' Then, in a
whisper: 'Because they think I'm dead.'

In a spasm of laughter, he rocked back into the divan, shaking
helplessly, 'Oh, my God, Kerans! What's the matter with you two?
Come out of that trance.' He looked up as Big Caesar approached,
doffing the dried alligator's head which he wore like a hood over
his own. 'Yes, what is it? A special song for Doctor Kerans? Capital! Did you hear that, Doctor? Let's go then, with *The Ballad of
Mistah Bones!*'

Clearing his throat, with much prancing and gesticulation,
the big Negro began, his voice deep and guttural.

> 'Mistah Bones, he loves dried men,
> Got himself a banana girl; three prophets sly,
> She played him all crazy, drowned him in the snake
>   wine,
> Never heard so many swamp birds,
> That old boss alligator.

> Rum Bones, he went skull fishing,
> Down off Angel Creek, where the dried men run,
> Took out his turtle stone, waited for the chapel boat,
> Three prophets landing.
> Some bad joss.

> Rum Bones, he saw the loving girl,
> Gave his turtle stone for two bananas,
> He had that banana girl like a hot mangrove;
> Prophets saw him,
> No dried men coming for Rum Bones.

> Rum Bones, he danced for that loving girl,
> Built a banana house for her loving bed—'

With a sudden shout, Strangman leapt from the divan, raced past Big Caesar into the centre of the square, pointing up at the perimeter wall of the lagoon high above them. Outlined against the setting sky was the small square figure of Dr. Bodkin, picking his way slowly across the wooden barrage that held back the creek waters outside. Unaware that he had been seen by the party below, he carried a small wooden box in one hand, a faint light fizzing from a trailing wire.

Wide awake, Strangman bellowed: 'Admiral! Big Caesar! Get him! He's got a bomb!'

In a wild scramble the party dissolved, with the exception of Beatrice and Kerans everyone raced off across the square. Shotguns slammed left and right, and Bodkin paused uncertainly, the fuse wire sparking about his legs. Then he turned and began to edge back along the barrage.

Kerans jumped to his feet and ran after the others. As he reached the perimeter wall star-shells were bursting into the air, spitting magnesium fragments across the roadway. Strangman and the Admiral were leaping up a fire escape, Big Caesar's shotgun slamming out over their heads. Bodkin had left the bomb in the centre of the dam and was racing away over the roof-tops.

Straddling the final ledge, Strangman leapt up on to the barrage, in a dozen strides reached the bomb and kicked it out into the centre of the creek. As the splash died away a cheer of approval went up from those below. Catching his breath, Strangman buttoned his jacket, then slipped a short-barrelled .38 from his shoulder holster. A thin smile glittered on his face. Whipping on the cries of his followers, he set out after Bodkin as he scaled his way painfully up the pontoon of the testing station.

KERANS LISTENED numbly to the final shots, remembering Bodkin's warning and the possibility, for which he bore him no grudge as he had chosen to ignore it, of being swept away himself with Strangman and his crew. He walked slowly back to the square, where Beatrice still sat on the heap of cushions, the alligator head on the ground in front of her. As he reached her he heard the footsteps behind him slowing menacingly, a strange silence fall over the pack.

He swung around to see Strangman saunter forward, a smirk twisting his lips. Big Caesar and the Admiral were at his shoulder, their shot-guns exchanged for machetes. The rest of the crew fanned out in a loose semicircle, watching expectantly, obviously pleased to see Kerans, the aloof medicine-man of a rival juju, get his just deserts.

'That was rather stupid of Bodkin, don't you think, Doctor? Dangerous too, as a matter of fact. We could damn' nearly have all been drowned.' Strangman paused a few feet from Kerans, eyeing him moodily. 'You knew Bodkin pretty well, I'm surprised you didn't anticipate that. I don't know whether I should take any more chances with mad biologists.'

He was about to gesture to Big Caesar when Beatrice jumped to her feet and rushed over to Strangman.

'Strangman! For heaven's sake, one's enough. Stop it. We won't hurt you! Look, you can have all these!'

With a wrench she unclasped the mass of necklaces, tore the tiaras from her hair and flung them at Strangman. Snarling with anger, Strangman kicked them into the gutter, and Big Caesar stepped past her, the machete swinging upward.

'Strangman!' Beatrice threw herself at Strangman, stumbled and almost dragged him to the ground by his lapels. 'You white devil, can't you leave us alone?'

Strangman twisted her away, breath seething through his clenched teeth. He gazed wildly at the dishevelled woman down on her knees among the jewels, and was about to wave Big Caesar on when a sudden intention tremor flickered across his right cheek. He slapped at it with his open hand, trying to brush it away like a fly, then flexed his facial muscles in an ugly grimace, unable to master the spasm. For a moment his face was twisted in a grotesque gape, like a man struggling in lock-jaw. Aware of his master's indecision, Big Caesar hesitated, and Kerans moved backwards into the shadows under the depot ship.

'All right! God, what a . . . !' Strangman muttered something thickly to himself and straightened his jacket, the point grudgingly conceded. The tic had faded. He nodded slowly at Beatrice, as if warning her that any future intercessions would be ignored, then barked sharply at Big Caesar. The machetes were tossed aside, but before Beatrice could protest again the entire pack threw itself on Kerans with a series of whoops and yells, hands flailing and clapping.

Kerans tried to sidestep them, uncertain from the circle of grinning faces whether this was merely some elaborate form of horseplay intended to discharge the tension that Bodkin's murder had generated, and at the same time administer a salutary reproof. He skipped around Strangman's divan as the pack closed in, found his escape blocked by the Admiral, who was feinting from side to side in his white tennis shoes like a dancer. Suddenly he sprang forwards and kicked Kerans' feet from under him. Kerans sat down heavily on the divan, and a dozen, oily brown-skinned arms seized him around the neck and shoulders and somersaulted him backwards on to the cobbled ground. He struggled helplessly to free himself, had a glimpse through the panting bodies of Strangman and Beatrice watching from the distance. Taking her arm, Strangman drew her firmly towards the gangway.

Then a large silk cushion was stuffed into Kerans' face, and hard palms began to pound a drum-beat across the back of his neck.

12

THE FEAST OF SKULLS

'THE FEAST OF SKULLS!'

Goblet raised in the flare-light, its amber contents spilling over his suit, Strangman let out an exultant shout, with a flourish leapt down from the fountain as the tumbril cart swerved across the cobbled square. Propelled by six sweating, bare-chested sailors bent double between its shafts, it rattled and jolted through the quickening embers of the charcoal fires, a dozen hands helping it on its way, and to a final accelerating crescendo on the drums struck the edge of the dais and tipped its white gleaming cargo across the boards at Kerans' feet. Immediately a chanting circle formed around him, hands beat out an excited rantando, white teeth flashed and snapped at the air like demoniac dice, hips swivelled and heels stamped. The Admiral dived forward and cleared a way through the whirling torsos, and Big Caesar, a steel trident held in front of him with a huge bale of red kelp and fucus transfixed on its barbs, lurched on to the dais and with a grunting heave tossed the dripping fronds into the air over the throne.

Kerans swayed forward helplessly as the sweet, acrid weeds cascaded around his head and shoulders, the lights of the dancing flares reflected in the gilt arm-rests of the throne. As the rhythm

of the drums beat around him, almost exorcising the deeper
pulse booming faintly in the base of his mind, he let his weight
hang against the leather thongs around his wrists, indifferent to
the pain as he sank in and out of consciousness. At his feet, at the
base of the throne, the broken white harvest of bones gleamed
with their ivory whiteness: slender tibias and femurs, scapulas
like worn trowels, a mesh of ribs and vertebrae, even two lolling
skulls. The light flickered across their bald pates and winked in
the empty eye sockets, leaping from the bowls of kerosene borne
by the corridor of statues which led towards the throne across the
square. The dancers had formed themselves into a long undulating line, and with Strangman prancing at their head began to
weave in and out of the marble nymphs, the drummers around
the fires pivotting in their seats to follow their progress.

Given a momentary respite as they circled the square, Kerans
lolled against the velvet back-rest, pulling automatically at his
clamped wrists. The kelp trailed around his neck and shoulders,
falling over his eyes from the tin crown Strangman had clamped
to his brow. Almost dry, the kelp exuded its sweaty stench, and
covered his arms so that only a few ragged strips of his dinner
jacket were visible. At the edge of the dais, beyond the litter of
bones and rum bottles, were more drifts of the weed, and a debris
of conches and dismembered starfish with which they had pelted
him before finding the mausoleum.

Twenty feet behind him towered the dark bulk of the depot
ship, a few lights still burning on its decks. For two nights
the parties had continued, the tempo mounting hour by hour,
Strangman apparently determined to exhaust his crew. Kerans
drifted helplessly in a half-conscious reverie, his pain dulled
by the rum forced down his throat (evidently the final indig-
nity, drowning Neptune in an even more magical and potent
sea), mild concussion cloaking the scene before him in a mist of
blood and scotomata. Dimly he was aware of his torn wrists and
bruised body, but he sat patiently, stoically acting out the role

of Neptune into which he had been cast, accepting the refuse and abuse heaped upon him as the crew discharged their fear and hatred of the sea. In that role, too, or its caricature which he performed, lay his only safety. Whatever his motives, Strangman still seemed reluctant to kill him, and the crew reflected this hesitation, always disguising their insults and tortures in the form of grotesque and hilarious jokes, protecting themselves when they pelted him with sea-weed by half-pretending to make an offering to an idol.

The snake of dancers reappeared and formed itself into a changing circle around him. Strangman detached himself from its centre—he was obviously reluctant to come too close to Kerans, perhaps afraid that the bleeding wrists and forehead would make him realise the crudity of the jape—and Big Caesar came forward, his huge knobbed face like an inflamed hippo's. Lumbering about to the rhythm of the bongos, he selected a skull and femur from the pile of bones around the throne, began to beat out a tattoo for Kerans, tapping the varying thicknesses of the temporal and occipital lobes to pick out a crude cranial octave. Several others joined in, and with a rattle of femur and tibia, radius and ulna, a mad dance of the bones ensued. Weakly, only half aware of the grinning, insulting faces pressed to within a foot or two of his own, Kerans waited for this to subside, then leaned back and tried to shield his eyes as a salvo of star-shells burst overhead and for a moment illuminated the depot ship and the surrounding buildings. This signalled the end of the festivity and the start of another night's work. With a shout, Strangman and the Admiral pulled apart the dancing group. The cart was hauled away, metal rims ringing over the cobbles, and the kerosene flares were extinguished. Within a minute the square was dark and empty, a few gutted fires sputtering among the cushions and drums, intermittently reflected in the gilt limbs of the throne and the white bones encircling it.

Now and then, at intervals through the night, a small group of looters would reappear, wheeling their booty in front of them, a bronze statue or a section of portico, hoist them into the ship and then vanish again, ignoring the motionless figure hunched on the throne among the shadows. By now Kerans was asleep, unaware of his fatigue and hunger, waking for a few minutes before dawn at the coolest ebb of the night to shout for Beatrice. He had not seen her since his capture after Bodkin's death, and assumed that Strangman had locked her away within the depot ship.

At last, after the exploding night with its bravura of drums and star-shells, the dawn lifted over the shadow-filled square, drawing behind it the immense golden canopy of the sun. Within an hour the square and the drained streets around it were silent, only a distant whir of an air-conditioner in the depot ship reminding Kerans that he was not alone. Somehow, by a manifest miracle, he had survived the previous day, sitting out unprotected in the full noon heat, shaded by only the cloak of weeds trailing from his crown. Like a stranded Neptune, he looked out from this pavilion of seaweed at the carpet of brilliant light covering the bones and garbage. Once he had been aware of a hatchway opening on to a deck above, and sensed that Strangman had come from his cabin to observe him—a few minutes later several buckets of icy water were tossed down on to him. He sipped feverishly at the cold drops falling from the weeds into his mouth like frozen pearls. Immediately afterwards he sank off into a profound torpor, waking after dusk just before the night's festivities were to begin.

Then Strangman had come down in his pressed white suit and examined him critically, in a strange access of pity suddenly murmured: 'Kerans, you're still alive. How do you do it?'

IT WAS THIS REMARK which sustained him through the second day, when the white carpet at noon lay over the square in incandescent layers a few inches apart, like the planes of parallel universes crystallised out of the continuum by the immense

heat. Across his skin the air burned like a flame. He stared listlessly at the marble statues, and thought of Hardman, moving
through the pillars of light on his way towards the mouth of the
sun, disappearing over the dunes of luminous ash. The same
power which guarded Hardman seemed to have revealed itself
within Kerans, in some way adjusting his metabolism so that
he could survive the unbroken heat. Still he was watched from
the deck above. Once a large salamander three feet long had
darted among the bones towards him, its insane teeth like flints
of obsidian flexing slowly as it scented Kerans, and a single shot
had roared out from the deck, smashing the lizard into a writhing bloodied mess at his feet.

Like the reptiles which sat motionlessly in the sunlight, he
waited patiently for the day to end.

Again Strangman seemed baffled to find him, swaying in
an exhausted delirium, but still alive. A flicker of nervousness
creased his mouth, and he glanced irritably at Big Caesar and
the crew waiting around the dais in the torchlight, apparently
as surprised as himself. When Strangman began to whoop and
shout for drums the response was markedly less prompt.

Determined to break Kerans' power for once and for all,
Strangman ordered two additional casks of rum lowered from the
depot-ship, hoping to drive from his men's minds their unconscious fear of Kerans and the paternal guardian of the sea he now
symbolised. Soon the square was filled with noisy stumbling figures, tipping their jugs and bottles to their lips, tap dancing on
the drum-skins. Accompanied by the Admiral, Strangman moved
swiftly from one party to another, inciting them to further acts of
extravagance. Big Caesar donned the alligator head and tottered
about the square on his knees, a whooping troupe of drummers
behind him.

Wearily Kerans waited for the climax. At Strangman's instructions the throne was lifted from the dais and lashed to the cart.
Kerans lay back limply against the head-rest, looking up at the

dark flanks of the buildings as Big Caesar heaped the bones and sea-weed around his feet. With a shout from Strangman the drunken procession set off, a dozen men fighting to get between the shafts of the tumbril, throwing it from left to right across the square and knocking down two of the statues. Amid a chorus of excited orders from Strangman and the Admiral, who raced along beside the wheels, trying helplessly to restrain it, the cart rapidly gathered speed and veered away into a side-street, careened along the pavement before demolishing a rusty lamp-standard. Bludgeoning the curly pates of the men around him with his massive fists, Big Caesar fought his way to the front of the shafts, seized one in each hand and enforced a more leisurely progress.

High above their heads, Kerans sat in the rocking throne, the cool air slowly reviving him. He watched the ceremony below with semi-conscious detachment, aware that they were moving systematically down every street in the drained lagoon, almost as if he were an abducted Neptune forced against his will to sanctify those sections of the drowned city which had been stolen from him by Strangman and reclaimed.

But gradually, as the exertion of pulling the cart cleared their heads and made them move in step, the men between the shafts began to sing what sounded like the lay of an old Haitian cargo cult, a deep crooning melody that again underlined their ambivalent attitude towards Kerans. In an effort to re-establish the real purpose of the outing, Strangman began to shout and brandish his flare pistol, after a short scrimmage made them reverse the direction of the cart so that they pushed it instead of pulled. As they passed the planetarium Big Caesar leapt up on to the cart, clinging to the throne like an immense ape, picked up the alligator's head and clamped it down over Kerans' shoulders.

Blinded and almost suffocated by the foetid stench of the crudely skinned hide, Kerans felt himself flung helplessly from side to side as the tumbril gained speed again. The men between the shafts, unaware of their direction, raced along the street, panting after Strangman and the Admiral, Big Caesar pursuing them with a rain of blows and kicks. Almost out of control, the cart swerved and lurched, narrowly missed wrecking itself on a traffic island, then straightened up and accelerated down an open stretch of roadway. As they neared a corner Strangman suddenly shouted to Big Caesar. Without looking, the huge mulatto flung his weight on the right-hand shaft and the cart pivoted and bounded up on to the sidewalk. For fifty yards it raced along helplessly, several of the men tripping over each other's legs and falling to the ground, then in a scream of axle iron and timber collided with the wall and pitched on to its side.

Torn from its mooring, the throne was flung half-way across the street into a low mud bank. Kerans lay face downwards, his impact with the ground softened by the damp silt, freed of the alligator head, but still trapped in his seat. Two or three of the crew were spread-eagled around him and picked themselves up, and an upended wheel of the cart rumbled slowly in the air.

Staggering helplessly with laughter, Strangman slapped Big Caesar and the Admiral on the back, soon had the rest of the crew jabbering excitedly to each other. They gathered around the wrecked cart, then went over to look at the upturned throne. Strangman rested one foot upon it majestically, rocking the shattered head-rest. Holding the pose long enough to convince his followers that Kerans' power was now truly spent, he holstered his flare pistol and ran away down the street, beckoning the others after him. With a chorus of jeers and shouts, the pack made off.

PINIONED BELOW the inverted throne, Kerans stirred painfully. His head and right shoulder were half buried in the bank of caking silt. He flexed his wrists against the loosened thongs, but they were still too tight for him to free his hands.

Shifting his weight on to his shoulders, he tried to pull the throne over by his arms, then noticed that the left-hand armrest had snapped from its vertical support. Slowly he pressed his blunted fingers under the arm-rest and began to work the thongs loop by loop over the ragged stump of the support protruding from the mortice joint.

When his hand freed itself, he let it fall limply to the ground, then massaged his bruised lips and cheeks, and kneaded the stiffened muscles of his chest and stomach. He twisted himself on to his side and picked at the knot clamping his right wrist to the other rest, in the brief flares of light from the star-shells loosened the thongs and freed himself.

For five minutes he lay inertly under the dark hulk of the throne, listening to the distant voices recede into the alleys beyond the depot ship. Gradually the flares faded, and the street became a silent canyon, the roof-tops faintly illuminated by the fading phosphorescent glow of the dying animalcula, which cast a web-like silver veil over the drained buildings and turned them into the expiring corner of an ancient spectral city.

Crawling from below the throne, he rose uncertainly to his feet, stumbled across the sidewalk and leaned against the wall, his head pounding from the exertion. He pressed his face against the cool still-damp stone, staring down the street into which Strangman and his men had disappeared.

Abruptly, before his eyes closed involuntarily, he saw two figures approaching, one familiarly white-suited, the other tall and bow-shouldered, walking swiftly down the street towards him.

'Strangman . . . !' Kerans whispered. His fingers gripped the loose mortar, and he stiffened into the shadows which covered the wall. The two men were a hundred yards away, but he could see Strangman's brisk, purposive stride, Big Caesar's loping step behind him. Something gleamed as it caught a ray of light shining down an intersection, a stab of silver that swung from Big Caesar's hand.

Searching the darkness, Kerans edged along the wall, almost cut his hands on a ragged angle of plate glass in a store window. A few yards away was the entrance to a large arcade, run-

ning through the block until it joined a parallel street fifty yards
to the west. Black silt a foot deep covered its floor, and Kerans
crouched down as he climbed the shallow steps, then ran slowly
through the dark tunnel to the far end of the arcade, the soft silt
muffling his limping footsteps.

He waited behind a pillar at the rear entrance, steadying
himself as Strangman and Big Caesar reached the throne. The
machete in the mulatto's giant hand seemed little more than a
razor. Strangman raised one hand warningly before touching the
throne. Carefully he scanned the streets and walls of windows, his
lean white jaw illuminated in the moonlight. Then he gestured
sharply at Big Caesar and kicked the throne over with his foot.

As their oaths rang out into the air, Kerans drew himself back
behind the pillar, then tiptoed quickly across the street towards
a narrow alleyway that ran off into the labyrinthine nexus of the
University quarter.

HALF AN HOUR LATER he took up his position on the top floor
of a fifteen-storey office block that formed part of the perimeter wall of the lagoon. A narrow balcony ringed the suite of
offices, at its rear leading to a fire escape that trailed off across
the lower roofs into the jungle beyond, finally swallowed by the
giant retaining banks of silt. Thin pools of water which had condensed from the afternoon heat mists lay across the plastic floors,
and after climbing the central stairwell Kerans lay down and
bathed his face and mouth in the cool liquid, slowly soothing his
wounded wrists.

No search-party came after him. Rather than concede complete defeat—the only interpretation most of the crew would put
upon Kerans' disappearance, Strangman had evidently decided to
accept his escape as a fait accompli and forget him, assuming that
Kerans would set off for the lagoons in the south. Through the
night the looting parties continued to rove the streets, each suc-
ceeding find signalised by a display of rockets and pyrotechnics.

Kerans rested until dawn, lying in a pool of water, letting it soak through the ragged strips of the silk dinner jacket that still clung to him, washing away the stench of the sea-weed and silt. An hour before dawn he pulled himself to his feet, tore off his jacket and shirt and stuffed them down a crack in the wall. He unscrewed a glass light bracket that was intact, carefully scooped up the water from one of the clean pools on the floor below. He had collected about a quart by the time the sun was lifting over the eastern perimeter of the lagoon. Two corridors down he trapped a small lizard in the washroom, killed it with a loose brick. He lit a fire of tinder with a lens of chipped glass, roasted the fillets of dark stringy meat until they were tender. The small steaks melted in his cracked mouth with the exquisite tenderness of warm fat. Recovering his strength, he climbed back to the top floor and retired to a service cubicle behind the elevator shaft. After wedging the door with a few lengths of rusty banister rail, he settled down in the corner and waited for the evening.

THE LAST SUNLIGHT was fading over the water as Kerans paddled his raft below the fronds of the fern trees dipping into the water around the lagoon, the blood and copper bronzes of the afternoon sun giving way to deep violets and indigo. Overhead the sky was an immense funnel of sapphire and purple, fantasticated whorls of coral cloud marking the descent of the sun like baroque vapour trails. A slack oily swell disturbed the surface of the lagoon, the water clinging to the leaves of the ferns like translucent wax. A hundred yards away it slapped lazily against the shattered remains of the jetty below the Ritz, throwing up a few broken spars of timber. Still restrained by the loose net of mooring lines, the fifty-gallon drums floated together like a group of humpbacked alligators. Luckily, the alligators Strangman had posted around the lagoon were still in their nests among the buildings, or had dispersed into the neighbouring creeks in search of food as the iguanas retreated before them.

Kerans paused before paddling out across the exposed face of the derelict bank adjacent to the Ritz, scanning the shoreline and the exit creek for any of Strangman's sentries. The concentration needed to build the raft from two galvanised iron water tanks had almost drained his brain, and he waited carefully before pushing on. As he neared the jetty he saw that the mooring lines had been slashed deliberately, the wooden box frame crushed by some heavy water-craft, probably the hydroplane, which Strangman had berthed in the central lagoon.

Wedging the raft between two of the floating drums, where it floated unobtrusively among the shifting debris, Kerans pulled himself up on to the balcony and stepped over the window-ledge into the hotel. Quickly he made his way up the staircase, following the trail of huge blurred footprints on the blue carpet mould which led down from the roof.

The penthouse had been wrecked. As he opened the outer wooden door into the suite a ragged glass panel of the interior air-seal fell to the floor at his feet. Someone had moved through the rooms in a berserk frenzy of violence, systematically smashing everything within sight. The Louis Quinze furniture had been hacked to pieces, dismembered legs and arms hurled through the internal glass walls. The carpeting over the floor lay in a tangle of long torn strips, even the cord underlay ripped apart so that the floor seals could be hacked and breached. Its legs lopped, the cabinet of the desk lay in two divided sections, the crocodile skin pared from its edges. Books were scattered underfoot, many of them slashed cleanly into two. A rain of blows had fallen upon the mantelpiece, huge gouges cut into its gilt lip, and enormous stars of frosted glass and silverscreen burst across the mirror like frozen explosions.

Stepping over the litter, Kerans ventured briefly on to the terrace, where the wire mesh of the mosquito screen had been ballooned outwards until it burst. The beach chairs where he had lain for so many months were chopped to matchwood.

As he expected, the decoy safe behind the desk had been sprung, its door open on the empty vault. Kerans went into the bedroom, a faint smile crossing his face when he realised that Strangman's house-breakers had failed to find the deep safe behind the bedroom mirror over the escritoire. The dented cylinder of the brass compass he had idly stolen from the base, still pointing to its talismanic south, lay on the floor below the small circular mirror, which it had shattered into a pattern like a magnified snow-flake. Kerans carefully rotated the rococo frame, released the hinge and drew it back to reveal the unbreached dial of the safe.

Darkness fell from the sky, throwing long shadows into the suite as Kerans' fingers raced through the tumblers. With a relieved intake of breath he pulled back the door, quickly slipped out the heavy Colt .45 and its carton of slugs. He sat down on the wrecked bed and tore the seals off the carton, then loaded the chamber, weighing the massive black weapon in his hand. He emptied the carton and filled his pockets with the slugs, then tightened his belt and went back into the lounge.

As he surveyed the room, he realised that by a curious paradox he bore Strangman little malice for wrecking the suite. In a sense its destruction, and with it all his memories of the lagoon, merely underlined something he had been tacitly ignoring for some time, and which Strangman's arrival, and all it implied, should have made him accept—the need to abandon the lagoon and move southwards. His time there had outlived itself, and the air-sealed suite with its constant temperature and humidity, its supplies of fuel and food, were nothing more than an encapsulated form of his previous environment, to which he had clung like a reluctant embryo to its yoke sac. The shattering of this shell, like the piercing doubts about his true unconscious motives set off by his near drowning in the planetarium, was the necessary spur to action, to his emergence into the brighter day of the interior, archaeopsychic sun. Now he would have to go forward.

Both the past, represented by Riggs, and the present contained within the demolished penthouse, no longer offered a viable existence. His commitment to the future, so far one of choice and plagued by so many doubts and hesitations, was now absolute.

IN THE DARKNESS the sleek curved hull of the depot ship rose into the air like the velvet belly of a stranded whale. Kerans crouched down in the shadow of the stern paddle, his lean bronzed body merging him into the background. He hid in the narrow interval between two of the blades, each a riveted metal slab fifteen feet wide and four feet deep, peering through the coconut-sized links of the drive chain. It was shortly before midnight, and the last of the foraging parties was leaving the gangway, the sailors, bottle in one hand and machete in the other, lurching off across the square. The cobbles were littered with burst cushions and bongo drums, bones and burnt-out embers, all kicked about in a careless mêlée.

Kerans waited until the last of the group made their way off among the streets, then stood up and secured the Colt in his belt. Far away, on the opposite side of the lagoon, was Beatrice's apartment, its windows in darkness, the light on the pylon extinguished. Kerans had considered climbing the stairs to the top floor, but safely assumed that Beatrice would be aboard the depot ship, an unwilling house-guest of Strangman.

Overhead a figure appeared at the rail, then withdrew. Distantly a voice shouted something, another replied from the bridge. A hatchway from the galley opened and a pailfull of filthy slops were tossed down into the square. Already a substantial pool of abyssal fluid had gathered under the ship; soon it would fill the lagoon and the ship would float again away.

Ducking under the band of the drive chain, Kerans stepped up on to the lowest blade, quickly pulled himself hand over hand up this curved radial ladder. The paddle creaked slightly, rotating a few inches under his weight as the slack in the drive chain was

taken in. At the top he transferred to the steel boom which carried the paddle axle. Steadying himself on the overhead guy-rope
controlling the blade-scraper, he crawled slowly along the foot-
wide boom, then stood up and climbed over the passenger rail
into the small well of the flag-deck. A narrow companionway led
up diagonally to the observation deck. Kerans scaled it soundlessly, pausing as he passed the two intervening decks in case any
sailor with a hangover was moon-gazing at the rail.

Hiding in the lee of a white-painted gig berthed on the deck,
Kerans moved forward, ducking from one ventilator to the next,
reached a rusty winch which stood a few feet from the dining
table where Strangman had entertained them. The table had
been stripped, the divans and chesterfield drawn up in a row
below the giant painting still propped against the funnels.

Voices sounded below again, and the gangway creaked as a
last departure stepped down into the square. In the distance, over
the roof-tops, a signal flare glowed briefly against the chimney
stacks. As it faded Kerans stood up and walked past the painting
towards the hatchway hidden behind it.

Suddenly he stopped, hand reaching for the butt of the Colt.
Little more than fifteen feet away from him, on the berthing
wing of the bridge, the red end of a cheroot glowed in the darkness, apparently detached from any corporeal form. Poised on the
balls of his feet, and unable to either move forward or withdraw,
Kerans searched the darkness around the glow, then picked out
the white brim of the Admiral's peaked cap. A moment later,
as he inhaled contentedly on the cheroot, the gleam of his eyes
reflected the glowing tip.

While the men below crossed the square, the Admiral turned
and surveyed the observation deck. Over the edge of the wooden
rail Kerans could see the butt of a shot-gun cradled loosely in
his elbow. The cheroot swivelled to one side of his mouth and
a cone of white smoke dispersed in the air like silver dust. For
a full two or three seconds he looked straight at Kerans, silhou-

etted in the darkness against the mass of figures on the canvas, but he gave no hint of recognition, apparently assuming that Kerans was part of the composition. Then he strolled slowly into the bridgehouse.

Picking each footstep carefully, Kerans advanced to the edge of the painting, then ducked into the shadows behind it. A fan of light from the hatchway lay across the deck. Crouching down, the Colt steady in his hand, he slowly descended the steps on to the empty gaming deck, watching the doorways for any sign of movement, for a levelled gun barrel among the curtains. Strangman's suite was directly below the bridge, entered by a panel door in an alcove behind the bar.

He waited by the door until a metal tray slammed in the galley, then leaned on the handle and eased the door off its latch, stepped silently into the darkness. For a few seconds he paused inside the door, adjusting his eyes to the dim light cast into the ante-room through a bead curtain hidden behind a chart cabinet on his right. In the centre of the room was a large map table, roll-maps under the glass top. His bare feet sank into the soft carpeting, and he stepped past the cabinet and peered through the beads.

The room, some 30 feet long, was Strangman's principal saloon, an oak-lined chamber with leather couches facing each other down the side walls, a large antique globe on its bronze pedestal below the forward row of portholes. Three chandeliers hung from the ceiling, but only one was lit, over a high-backed Byzantine chair with stained-glass inlays at the far end of the room, shining on the jewels which spilled from the metal gun-boxes drawn up on a semicircle of low tables.

Head back against the chair, one hand touching the slender stem of a gold-lipped glass on a mahogany table at her elbow, was Beatrice Dahl. Her blue brocade dress was spread out like a peacock's tail, a few pearls and sapphires which had spilled from her left hand gleaming among the folds like electric eyes.

Kerans hesitated, watching the door opposite which led into Strangman's cabin, then parted the curtain slightly so that the beads tinkled gently.

Beatrice ignored this, obviously too-familiar with the sound of rustling glass. The chests at her feet were loaded with a mass of jewelled trash—diamanté anklets, gilt clasps, tiaras and chains of zircon, rhinestone necklaces and pendants, huge ear-rings of cultured pearl, overflowing from one chest to another and spilling on to the salvers placed on the floor like vessels to catch a quicksilver rainfall.

For a moment Kerans thought that Beatrice had been drugged—her expression was vacant and blank, like the mask of a wax dummy, her eyes on some distant focus. Then her hand moved, and she raised the wine glass perfunctorily to her lips.

'Beatrice!'

With a start she tipped the wine across her lap, looked up in surprise. Pushing back the beads, Kerans stepped quickly across the room, caught her elbow as she began to rise from the chair.

'Beatrice, wait! Don't move yet!' He tried the door behind the chair, found it locked. 'Strangman and his men are looting the streets, I think there's only the Admiral up on the bridge.'

Beatrice pressed her face to his shoulders, with her cool fingers traced the black bruises showing through his bronzed skin. 'Robert, be careful! What happened to you? Strangman wouldn't let me watch!' Her relief and pleasure at seeing Kerans gave way to alarm. She glanced anxiously around the room. 'Darling, leave me here and get away. I don't think Strangman will harm me.'

Kerans shook his head, then helped her to her feet. He gazed at Beatrice's elegant profile, at her sleek carmine mouth and lacquered nails, almost bemused by the heady scent of perfume and the brocaded rustle of her gown. After the violence and filth of the past days he felt like one of the dust-begrimed discoverers of the tomb of Nefertiti stumbling upon her exquisite painted mask in the depths of the necropolis.

'Strangman's capable of anything, Beatrice. He's insane. They were playing a sort of mad game with me, very nearly killed me.'

Beatrice gathered the train of her skirt, brushing away the jewels that clung to its fabric. Despite the lavish assortment before her, her wrists and breast were bare, one of her own small gold clasps in a contoured twist around her neck. 'But Robert, even if we get out—'

'Quiet!' Kerans stopped a few feet from the curtain, watching the strands balloon faintly and then subside, trying to remember whether there was a porthole open in the anteroom. 'I've built a small raft, it should carry us far enough. Later we'll rest and build a larger one.'

He started to walk towards the curtain when two of the strands parted fractionally, something moved with snake-like speed and a whirling silver blade three feet long cleft the air and spun towards his head like an immense scythe. Wincing with pain, Kerans ducked and felt the blade skim past his right shoulder, tearing a shallow three-inch weal, then impale itself with a steely shudder in the oak panelling behind him. Voice frozen in her throat, Beatrice backed wild-eyed into one of the occasional tables, knocking a chest of jewels across the floor.

Before Kerans could reach her the curtain was thrashed back by an enormous arm and a huge hunch-backed figure filled the doorway, his one-eyed head lowered like a bull's below the transom. Sweat poured from his huge muscled chest, staining his green shorts. In his right hand was a twelve-inch barb of gleaming steel, about to thrust upwards at Kerans' stomach.

Side-stepping down the room, Kerans steadied the revolver in his hands, the huge Negro's single cyclopean eye following him. Then he stepped on the open teeth of a necklace clasp, involuntarily stumbled back against a sofa.

As he steadied himself against the wall Big Caesar launched himself through the air at Kerans, the knife driving through the air in a short arc like the tip of a propeller. Beatrice screamed, her

voice abruptly drowned in the tremendous roar of the Colt. Jolted
by the recoil, Kerans sat down in the sofa, watched the mulatto
crash crookedly against the doorway, the knife spilling from his
hand. A strangled bubbling grunt erupted from his throat, and
with a cataclysmic wrench which seemed to sum up all his pain
and frustration he tore at the bead curtain and ripped it from the
transom. The bunching muscles of his torso contracted for the
last time. Draped in the curtain, he fell forward on to the floor,
his vast limbs like a bloated giant's, the thousands of beads spilling around him.

'Beatrice! Come on!' Kerans seized her arm, steered her past
the prostrate body into the ante-room, his right hand and fore-
arm numb from the jarring discharge of the Colt. They crossed
the alcove, and raced past the deserted bar. Overhead a voice
shouted from the bridge, and footsteps hurried across the deck
to the rail.

Kerans stopped, looking down at the voluminous folds of Beatrice's gown, then abandoned his plan to retrace his entry over
the stern paddle.

'We'll have to try the gangway.' He pointed to the unguarded
entrance by the starboard rail, the beckoning night-club cupids
with flutes to their ruby lips dancing on either side of the steps. 'It
may look a little obvious, but it's just about the only way left now.'

Half-way down, the gangway began to rock in its davits, and
they heard the Admiral bark down at them :from the bridge.
A moment later the shot-gun roared out, the pellets slashing
through the clapboard roof over their heads. Kerans ducked, at
the mouth of the gangway craned up at the bridge, now directly
overhead, saw the long barrel of the shot-gun sticking into the
air as the Admiral manoeuvred about.

Kerans jumped down into the square, took Beatrice by the waist
and swung her down. Together they crouched under the hull of
the depot ship, then darted across the square to the nearest street.

Half-way there Kerans looked over his shoulder as a group of

Strangman's men appeared on the far side of the square. They shouted to and fro with the Admiral then spotted Kerans and Beatrice a hundred yards away.

Kerans started to run on, the revolver still clasped in his hand, but Beatrice held him back.

'No, Robert! Look!'

In front of them, stretched arm to arm across the full width of the street, another group approached, a white-suited man at its centre. He strolled along, one thumb hooked casually into his belt, the other signalling his men on, his fingers almost touching the tip of the machete brandished by the man next to him.

Changing direction, Kerans pulled Beatrice diagonally across the square, but the first group had fanned out and cut them off. A star-shell went up from the deck of the ship and illuminated the square in its roseate light.

Beatrice stopped, out of breath, helplessly holding the broken heel of her gold slipper. She looked uncertainly at the men closing in on them. 'Darling . . . Robert—what about the ship? Try to get back there yourself.'

Kerans took her arm and they backed into the shadows below the forward paddle, hidden by the blades from the shot-gun on the bridge. The exertion of climbing aboard the ship and then running about the square had exhausted Kerans, and his lungs pumped in painful spasms, so that he could barely steady the revolver.

'Kerans. . . .' Strangman's cool, ironic voice drifted across the square. He advanced at a relaxed amble, just within range of the Colt but well screened by the men on either side of him. All carried machetes and pangas, their faces amiable and unhurried.

'Finis, Kerans . . . Finis.' Strangman stopped twenty feet from Kerans, his sardonic lips wreathed in a soft smile, surveying him with almost kindly pity. 'Sorry, Kerans, but you're being a bit of a nuisance. Throw away the gun or we'll kill the Dahl girl, too.' He waited for a few seconds.

'I mean it.'

Kerans found his voice. 'Strangman—'

'Kerans, this is no time for a metaphysical discussion.' A note of annoyance crept into his voice, as if he were dealing with a fractious child. 'Believe me, no time for prayers, no time for anything. I told you to drop the gun. Then walk forward. My men think you abducted Miss Dahl; they won't touch her.' He added, with a touch of menace: 'Come on, Kerans. We don't want anything to happen to Beatrice, do we? Think what a beautiful mask her face will make.' He tittered insanely. 'Better than that old alligator you wore.'

Phlegm choking his throat, Kerans swung around and handed the revolver to Beatrice, pressing her small hands around the butt. Before their eyes could meet he looked away, inhaling for the last time the musky perfume on her breasts, then began to walk out into the square as Strangman had ordered. The latter watched him with an evil smirk, then suddenly leapt forward with a snarl, whipping the others on.

As the long knives lanced through the air after him Kerans turned and raced around the paddle, trying to reach the area behind the ship. Then his feet slipped in one of the foetid pools, before he could catch himself he fell heavily. He scrambled to his knees, one arm raised helplessly to ward off the circle of raised machets, then felt something seize him from behind and roughly pull him backwards off balance.

Recovering his foothold on the damp cobbles, he heard Strangman shout in surprise. A group of brown-uniformed men, rifles at their hips, stepped rapidly from the shadows behind the depot ship where they had been hiding. At their head was the trim, brisk figure of Colonel Riggs. Two of the soldiers carried a light machine-gun, a third man two boxes of belt ammunition. They quickly set it up on its tripod ten feet in front of Kerans, levelled the perforated, air-cooled barrel at the confused mob backing away from them. The rest of the soldiers fanned out in a widening semicircle, prodding the slower of Strangman's men with their bayonets.

Most of the crew were shambling backwards in the general melee across the square, but a couple of them, still holding their pangas, attempted to break through the cordon. Instantly there was a short decisive volley of shots over their heads, and they dropped their knives and fell back mutely with the rest.

'Okay, Strangman. That will do very nicely.' Riggs rapped his baton across the Admiral's chest and forced him back.

Completely disconcerted by all this, Strangman gaped blankly at the soldiers swarming past him. He searched the depot ship helplessly, as if expecting some large siege cannon to be wheeled forward and reverse the situation. Instead, however, two helmeted soldiers appeared on the bridge with a portable searchlight, swivelled its beam down into the square.

Kerans felt someone take his elbow. He looked round at the solicitous beak-like face of Sergeant Macready, a submachinegun in the crook of his arm. At first he almost failed to identify Macready, only with an effort managed to place his aquiline features, like a face dimly remembered across the span of a lifetime.

'You all right, sir?' Macready asked softly. 'Sorry to jerk you about like that. Looks as if you've been having a bit of a party here.'

13

TOO SOON, TOO LATE

BY EIGHT O'CLOCK the next morning Riggs had stabilised the situation and was able to see Kerans informally. His headquarters were in the testing station, with a commanding view over the streets below, and particularly of the paddle-ship in the square. Stripped of their weapons, Strangman and his crew sat around in the shade under the hull, supervised by the light machine-gun manned by Macready and two of his men.

Kerans and Beatrice had spent the night in the sick-bay aboard Riggs' patrol cruiser, a well-armed 30-ton PT boat which was now moored against the hydroplane in the central lagoon. The unit had arrived shortly after midnight, and a reconnaissance patrol reached the testing station on the perimeter of the drained lagoon at about the time Kerans entered Strangman's suite in the depot ship. Hearing the ensuing gunfire, they descended immediately into the square.

'I guessed Strangman was here,' Riggs explained. 'One of our aerial patrols reported seeing the hydroplane about a month ago, and I reckoned you might have a little trouble with him if you were still hanging on. The pretext of trying to reclaim the testing station was a fair one.' He sat on the edge of the desk, watching the helicopter circle the open streets. 'That should keep them quiet for a bit.'

'Daley seems to have found his wings at last,' Kerans commented.

'He's had a lot of practice.' Riggs turned his intelligent eyes on Kerans, asked casually: 'By the way, is Hardman here?'

'Hardman?' Kerans shook his head slowly. 'No; I haven't seen him since the day he disappeared. He'll be a long way off by now, Colonel.'

'You're probably right. I just thought he might be around.' He flashed Kerans a sympathetic smile, evidently having forgiven him for scuttling the testing station, or sensible enough not to press the matter so soon after Kerans' ordeal. He pointed to the streets below glowering in the sunlight, the dry silt on the roof-tops and walls like caked dung. 'Pretty grim down there. Damn' shame about old Bodkin. He really should have come north with us.'

Kerans nodded, looking across the office at the machete scars sliced into the woodwork around the door, part of the damage gratuitously inflicted on the station after Bodkin's death. Most of the mess had been cleaned up, and his body, lying among the bloodstained programme charts in the laboratory below, flown out to the patrol cruiser. To his surprise, Kerans realised that callously he had already forgotten Bodkin and felt little more than a nominal pity for him. Riggs' mention of Hardman had reminded him of something far more urgent and important, the great sun still beating magnetically within his mind, and a vision of the endless sandbanks and blood-red swamps of the south passed before his eyes.

He went over to the window, picking a splinter from the sleeve of his fresh uniform jacket, and stared down at the men huddled under the depot ship. Strangman and the Admiral had gone forward towards the machine-gun, and were remonstrating with Macready, who was shaking his head impassively.

'Why don't you arrest Strangman?' he asked.

Riggs laughed shortly. 'Because there's absolutely nothing I

can hold him on. Legally, as he full well knows, he was absolutely entitled to defend himself against Bodkin, kill him if
necessary.' When Kerans looked round over his shoulder in surprise he continued: 'Don't you remember the Reclaimed Lands
Act and the Dykes Maintenance Regulations? They're still very
much in force. I know Strangman's a nasty piece of work—with
that white skin and his alligators—but strictly speaking he
deserves a medal for pumping out the lagoon. If he complains,
I'll have a job explaining that machine-gun down there. Believe
me Robert, if I'd arrived five minutes later and found you
chopped to bits Strangman could have claimed that you were an
accomplice of Bodkin's and I'd have been able to do nothing. He's
a clever fellow.'

Tired out after only three hours' sleep, Kerans leaned against
the window, smiling wanly to himself as he tried to resolve
Riggs' tolerant attitude towards Strangman with his own expe-
riences of the man. He was conscious that an even wider gulf
now divided Riggs and himself. Although the Colonel was only
a few feet away from him, emphasising his argument with brisk
flourishes of the baton, he was unable to accept wholly the idea
of Riggs' reality, almost as if his image were being projected into
the testing station across enormous distances of time and space
by some elaborate three-dimensional camera. It was Riggs, and
not himself, who was the time-traveller. Kerans had noticed a
similar lack of physical validity about the rest of the crew. Many
of the original members had been replaced—all those, among
them Wilson and Caldwell, who had begun to experience the
deep dreams. For this reason, perhaps—and partly because
of their pallid faces and weak eyes, in so marked contrast to
Strangman's men, the present crew seemed flat and unreal, moving about their tasks like intelligent androids.

'What about the looting?' he asked.

Riggs shrugged. 'Apart from a few trinkets filched from an old
Woolworths, he's taken nothing that couldn't be put down to nat-

ural exuberance on the part of his men. As for all the statues and
so on, he's doing a valuable job reclaiming works of art that were
perforce abandoned. Though I'm not sure what his real motives
are.' He patted Kerans on the shoulder. 'You'll have to forget
about Strangman, Robert. The only reason he's sitting quiet now
is that he knows he's got the law on his side. If he hadn't there'd
be a battle royal going on.' He broke off. 'You look all in, Robert.
Are you still getting these dreams?'

'Now and then.' Kerans shuddered. 'The last few days have
been insane here. It's difficult to describe Strangman—he's like
a white devil out of a voodoo cult. I can't accept the idea that he'll
go scot free. When are you going to re-flood the lagoon?'

'Re-flood the—?' Riggs repeated, shaking his head in bewil-
derment. 'Robert, you really are out of touch with reality. The
sooner you get away from here the better. The last thing I intend
to do is re-flood the lagoon. If anybody tries I'll personally blow
his head off. Reclaiming land, particularly an urban area like
this right in the centre of a former capital city, is a Class A1 pri-
ority. If Strangman is serious about pumping out the next two
lagoons he'll not only get a free pardon, but a governor-general-
ship to boot.' He looked down through the window, as the metal
rungs of the fire escape rang in the sunlight. 'Here he comes
now. I wonder what's on his evil little mind?'

Kerans went over to Riggs, averting his eyes from the maze of
festering yellow roof-tops. 'Colonel, you've got to flood it again,
laws or no laws. Have you been down in those streets; they're
obscene and hideous! It's a nightmare world that's dead and finished, Strangman's resurrecting a corpse! After two or three days
here you'll—'

Riggs swung away from the desk, cutting Kerans off. An element of impatience crept into his voice. 'I don't intend to stay
here for three days,' he snapped curtly. 'Don't worry. I'm not suffering from any crazy obsessions about these lagoons, flooded or
otherwise. We're leaving first thing tomorrow, all of us.'

Puzzled, Kerans said: 'But you can't leave, Colonel. Strangman will still be here.'

'Of course he will! Do you think that paddle-boat has got wings? There's no reason for him to leave, if he thinks he can take the big heat waves coming, and the rain-storms. You never know. If he gets a few of these big buildings refrigerated he may be able to. In time, if he reclaims enough of the city, there might even be an attempt to reoccupy it. When we get back to Byrd I'll definitely put in a formal recommendation. However, at present there's nothing for me to stay for—I can't move the station now, but it's a fair loss. Anyway, you and the Dahl girl need a rest. *And* a brain-lift. Do you realise how lucky she is to be in one piece? Good God!' He nodded sharply at Kerans, standing up as a firm rap sounded on the door. 'You should be grateful that I came here in time.'

Kerans walked over to the side door into the galley, eager to avoid Strangman. He paused for a moment to look up at Riggs. 'I don't know about that, Colonel. I'm afraid you came too late.'

14

GRAND SLAM

CROUCHED DOWN IN a small office two floors above the barrage, Kerans listened to the music playing amid the lights on the top deck of the depot ship. Strangman's party was still in full swing. Propelled by two junior members of the crew, the big paddles rotated slowly, their blades dividing the coloured spot lights and swinging them up into the sky. Seen from above, the white awnings resembled the marquee of a fairground, a brilliant focus of noise and festivity in the darkened square.

As a concession to Strangman, Riggs had joined him at this farewell party. A bargain had been struck between the two leaders; earlier the machine-gun had been withdrawn and the lower level placed out of bounds to the Colonel's men, while Strangman agreed to remain within the perimeter of the lagoon until Riggs had left. All day Strangman and his pack had roved the streets, and the random sounds of looting and firing echoed to and fro. Even now, as the last guests, the Colonel and Beatrice Dahl, left the party and climbed the fire escape to the testing station, fighting had broken out on deck and bottles were being hurled down into the square.

Kerans had put in a token appearance at the party, keeping well away from Strangman, who made little attempt to talk to him. At one point, between cabaret turns, he had swept past Kerans, deliberately brushing his elbow, and toasted him with his goblet.

'I hope you're not too bored, Doctor. You look tired. Ask the Colonel to lend you his punka-wallah.' He turned a wicked smile on Riggs, who was sitting erectly on a tasselled silk cushion with a circumspect expression on his face like a district commissioner at a pasha's court. 'The parties Dr. Kerans and I are used to are very different affairs, Colonel. They really go with a bang.'

'So I believe, Strangman,' Riggs replied mildly, but Kerans turned away, unable, like Beatrice, to mask his revulsion for Strangman. She was looking over her shoulder across the square, a small frown for a moment hiding the mood of torpor and self-immersion to which she was again returning.

Watching Strangman from the distance as he applauded the next cabaret turn, Kerans wondered whether in some way he had passed his peak, and was beginning to disintegrate. He now looked merely loathsome, like a decaying vampire glutted with evil and horror. The sometime charm had vanished, in its place a predatory gleam. As soon as he could, Kerans feigned a mild attack of malaria, and made his way out into the darkness and up the fire escape to the testing station.

Now determined on the only solution available, Kerans' mind felt clear and co-ordinated again, extending outwards beyond the perimeter of the lagoon.

Only fifty miles to the south, the rain-clouds were packed together in tight layers, blotting out the swamps and archipelagos of the horizon. Obscured by the events of the past week, the archaic sun in his mind beat again continuously with its immense power, its identity merging now with that of the real sun visible behind the rain-clouds. Relentless and magnetic, it called him southward, to the great heat and submerged lagoons of the Equator.

Assisted by Riggs, Beatrice climbed up on to the roof of the testing station, which also served as the helicopter landing stage. When Sergeant Daley started his engine and the rotors began to spin, Kerans quickly made his way down to the balcony two floors below. Separated by a hundred yards or so on either side, he was directly between the helicopter and the barrage, the continuous terrace of the building linking the three points.

Behind the building was an enormous bank of silt, reaching upwards out of the surrounding swamp to the railings of the terrace, on to which spilled a luxurious outcrop of vegetation. Ducking below the broad fronds of the fern-trees, he raced along to the barrage, fitted between the end of the building and the shoulder of the adjacent office block. Apart from the exit creek on the far side of the lagoon where the pumping scows had been stationed, this was the only major entry point for the water that had passed into the lagoon. The original inlet, once twenty yards wide and deep, had shrunk to a narrow channel clogged with mud and fungi, its six-foot-wide mouth blocked by a rampart of heavy logs. Initially, once the rampart was removed, the rate of flow would be small, but as more and more of the silt was carried away the mouth would widen again.

From a small cache below a loose flagstone he withdrew two square black boxes, each containing six sticks of dynamite lashed together. He had spent all afternoon searching through the nearby buildings for them, confident that Bodkin had raided the armoury of the base at the same time that he had stolen the compass; sure enough, he finally found the trove in an empty lavatory cistern.

As the helicopter engine began to fire more loudly, the exhaust spitting brightly into the darkness, he lit the short 30-second fuse, straddled the rail and ran out towards the centre of the barrage.

There he bent down and suspended the boxes from a small peg he had driven into the outer row of logs earlier that evening. They hung safely out of view, about two feet from the water's edge.

'Dr. Kerans! Get away from there, sir!'

Kerans looked up to see Sergeant Macready at the further end of the barrage, standing at the rail of the next roof. He leaned forward, suddenly spotting the flickering end of the fuse, then rapidly unslung his Thompson gun.

Head down, Kerans raced back along the barrage, reached the terrace as Macready shouted again and then fired a short burst. The slugs tore at the railings, gouging out pieces of the cement, and Kerans fell as one of the cupro-nickel bullets struck his right leg just above the ankle. Pulling himself over the rail, he saw Macready shoulder the gun and jump down on to the barrage.

'Macready! Go back!' he shouted to the Sergeant, who was loping along the wooden planks. 'It's going to blow!'

Backing away among the fronds, his voice lost in the roar of the helicopter as it carried out its take-off check, he helplessly watched Macready stop in the centre of the barrage and reach down to the boxes.

'Twenty-eight, twenty-nine. . . .' Kerans concluded automatically to himself. Turning his back on the barrage, he limped away down the terrace, then threw himself on to the floor.

AS THE TREMENDOUS roar of the explosion lifted up into the dark sky, the immense fountain of erupting foam and silt briefly illuminated the terrace, outlining Kerans' spread-eagled form. From an initial crescendo, the noise seemed to mount in a continuous sustained rumble, the breaking thunder of the shock wave yielding to the low rush of the bursting cataract. Clods of silt and torn vegetation spattered on the tiles around Kerans, and he stumbled to his feet and reached the rail.

Widening as he watched, the water jetted down into the open streets below, carrying with it huge sections of the silt bank. There was a concerted rush to the deck of the depot ship, a dozen arms pointing up at the water pouring out of the breach. It swilled into the square, only a few feet deep, blotting out the fires and splashing against the hull of the ship, still rocking slightly from the impact of the explosion.

Then, abruptly, the lower section of the barrage fell forwards, a brace of a dozen twenty-foot logs going down together. The U-shaped saddle of silt behind collapsed in turn, exposing the full bore of the inlet creek, and what appeared to be a gigantic cube of water fifty feet high tipped into the street below like a flopping piece of jelly. With a dull rumbling roar of collapsing buildings, the sea poured in full flood.

'Kerans!'

He turned as a shot whipped overhead, saw Riggs running forward from the helicopter landing stage, pistol in hand. His engine stalled, Sergeant Daley was helping Beatrice out of the cabin.

The building was shaking under the impact of the torrent sweeping past its shoulder. Supporting his right leg with his hand, Kerans hobbled into the lee of the small tower which had held his previous observation window. From his trouser belt he pulled the .45 Colt, held the butt in both hands and fired twice around the corner at the approaching hatless figure of Riggs. Both shots went wild, but Riggs stopped and backed off a few feet, taking cover behind a balustrade.

Feet moved quickly towards him and he looked around as Beatrice raced along the terrace. Reaching the corner as Riggs and Daley shouted after her, she sank down on her knees beside Kerans.

'Robert, you've got to leave! Now, before Riggs brings more of his men! He wants to kill you, I know.'

Kerans nodded, getting painfully to his feet. 'The Sergeant—I didn't realise he was patrolling. Tell Riggs I'm sorry—' He gestured helplessly, then took a last look at the lagoon. The black water surged across it through the buildings, level with the top line of their windows. Upended, its paddles stripped away, the depot ship drifted slowly towards the far shore, its hull sticking up into the air like the belly of an expiring whale. Spurts of steam and foam erupted from its exploding boilers, bursting out through the gashes in the hull as it was driven across the sharp reefs of the half-submerged cornices. Kerans watched it with a quiet contained pleasure, savouring the fresh tang that the water had brought again to the lagoon. Neither Strangman nor any members of his crew were visible, and the few fragments of splintered bridge and funnel swept away by the water were swallowed and regurgitated by the boiling undercurrents.

'Robert! Hurry!' Beatrice pulled his arm, glancing back over her shoulder at the darting figures of Riggs and the pilot only fifty yards away. 'Darling, where are you going. I'm sorry I can't be with you.'

'South,' Kerans said softly, listening to the roar of the deepening water. 'Towards the sun. You'll be with me, Bea.'

He embraced her, then tore himself from her arms and ran to the rear rail of the terrace, pushing back the heavy fern fronds. As he stepped down on to the silt bank Riggs and Sergeant Daley appeared around the corner and fired into the foliage, but Kerans ducked and ran away between the curving trunks, sinking up to his knees in the soft mud.

The edge of the swamp had receded slightly as the water poured away into the lagoon, and he painfully dragged the bulky catamaran, home-made from four fifty-gallon drums arranged in parallel pairs, through the thick rasp-weeds to the water. Riggs and the pilot emerged through the ferns as he pushed off.

While the outboard kicked into life he lay exhausted on the planking, the shots from Riggs' .38 cutting through the small triangular sail. Slowly the interval of water widened to a hundred and then two hundred yards, and he reached the first of the small islands that grew out of the swamp on the roofs of isolated buildings. Hidden by them, he sat up and reefed the sail, then looked back for the last time at the perimeter of the lagoon.

Riggs and the pilot were no longer visible, but high up on the tower of the building he could see the lonely figure of Beatrice, waving slowly towards the swamp, changing tirelessly from one arm to the other, although she was unable to distinguish him among the islands. Far to her right, rising up above the encompassing silt banks, were the other familiar landmarks he knew so well, even the green roof of the Ritz, fading into the haze. At last all he could see were the isolated letters of the giant slogan Strangman's men had painted, looming out of the darkness over the flat water like a concluding epitaph: Time Zone.

The opposing flow of water slowed his progress, and fifteen minutes later, when the helicopter roared over, he had still not reached the edge of the swamp. Passing the top floor of a small building, he glided in through one of the windows, waited quietly as the aircraft roared up and down, machine-gunning the islands.

When it left he pushed on again, within an hour finally navigated the exit waters of the swamp and entered the broad inland sea that would lead him to the south. Large islands, several hundred yards in length, covered its surface, their vegetation crowding out into the water, their contours completely altered by the rising water in the short period that had elapsed since their search for Hardman. Shipping the outboard, he set the small sail, made a steady two or three miles an hour tacking across the light southerly breeze.

His leg had begun to stiffen below the knee, and he opened the small medical kit he had packed and washed the wound in a penicillin spray, then bandaged it tightly. Just before dawn, when the pain became unbearable, he took one of the morphine tablets and fell off into a loud, booming sleep, in which the great sun expanded until it filled the entire universe, the stars themselves jolted by each of its beats.

HE WOKE AT SEVEN the next morning, lying back against the mast in bright sunlight, the medical kit open in his lap, the bows of the catamaran rammed lightly into a large fern-tree growing off the edge of a small island. A mile away, flying fifty feet above the water, the helicopter raced along, machine-gun fire flickering from its cabin at the islands below. Kerans shipped the mast and glided in under the tree, waiting until the helicopter left. Massaging his leg, but fearful of the morphine, he made a small meal of a bar of chocolate, the first of ten he had been able to collect. Luckily the petty officer in charge of stores aboard the patrol boat had been instructed to give Kerans free access to the medical supplies.

The aerial attacks were resumed at half-hour intervals, the aircraft once flying directly overhead. From his hiding place in one of the islands Kerans clearly saw Riggs looking out from the hatchway, his small jaw jutting fiercely. However, the machine-gun fire became more and more sporadic, and the flights were finally discontinued that afternoon.

By then, at five o'clock, Kerans was almost completely exhausted. The noon temperature of a hundred and fifty degrees had drained all energy from him, and he lay limply under the moistened sail, letting the hot water drip down on to his chest and face, praying for the cooler air of the evening. The surface of the water turned to fire, so that the craft seemed to be suspended on a cloud of drifting flame. Pursued by strange visions, he paddled feebly with one hand.

15

THE PARADISES OF THE SUN

THE NEXT DAY, by good luck, the storm-clouds moved over-head between himself and the sun, and the air grew markedly cooler, falling to ninety-five degrees at noon. The massive banks of black cumulus, only four or five hundred feet above, dimmed the air like a solar eclipse, and he revived sufficiently to start the outboard and raise his speed to ten miles an hour. Circling between the islands, he moved on southwards, following the sun that pounded in his mind. Later that evening, as the rain-storms lashed down, he felt well enough to stand up on one leg by the mast, letting the torrential bursts rain across his chest and strip away the ragged fabric of his jacket. When the first of the storm-belts moved off the visibility cleared, and he could see the southern edge of the sea, a line of tremendous silt banks over a hundred yards in height. In the spasmodic sunlight they glit-tered along the horizon like fields of gold, the tops of the jungle beyond rising above them.

Half a mile from the shore the reserve tank of the outboard ran dry. He unbolted the motor and threw it into the water, watched it sink through the brown surface in a faint wreath of bubbles. He furled the sail and paddled slowly against the head-breeze. By the time he reached the shore it was dusk, the shadows sweeping across the huge grey slopes. Limping through the shallows, he beached the craft, then sat down with his back against one of the drums. Staring out over the immense loneliness of this dead terminal beach, he soon fell into an exhausted sleep.

The next morning he dismantled the craft, ported the sections one by one up the enormous sludge-covered slopes, hoping for a southward extension of the waterway. Around him the great banks undulated for miles, the curving dunes dotted with cuttlefish and nautiloids. The sea was no longer visible, and he was alone with these few lifeless objects, like the debris of a vanished continuum, one dune giving way to another as he dragged the heavy fifty-gallon drums from crest to crest. Overhead the sky was dull and cloudless, a bland impassive blue, more the interior ceiling of some deep irrevocable psychosis than the storm-filled celestial sphere he had known during the previous days. At times, after he had dropped one burden, he would totter down into the hollow of the wrong dune, find himself stumbling about the silent basins, their floors cracked into hexagonal plates, like a dreamer searching for an invisible door out of his nightmare.

Finally he abandoned the craft and trudged on ahead with a small parcel of supplies, looking back as the drums sank slowly below the surface. Carefully avoiding the quicksands between the dunes, he moved on towards the jungle in the distance, where the green spires of the great horsetails and fern-trees reached a hundred feet into the air.

HE RESTED AGAIN below a tree on the edge of the forest, carefully cleaning his pistol. Ahead of him he could hear the bats screech and dive among the dark trunks in the endless twilight world of the forest floor, the iguanas snarl and lunge. His ankle had begun to swell painfully; the continual extension of the damaged muscle spread its original infection. Cutting a branch off one of the trees, he hobbled forward into the shadows.

By evening the rainfall started, slashing at the huge umbrellas a hundred feet above, the black light only broken when phosphorescent rivers of water broke and poured down on him. Frightened of resting for the night, he pressed on, shooting off the attacking iguanas, darting from the shelter of one massive tree-trunk to the next. Here and there he found a narrow breach in the canopy overhead, and a pale light would illuminate a small clearing where the ruined top floor of a sunken building loomed through the foliage, the rain beating across it. But the evidence of any man-made structures was increasingly scanty, the towns and cities of the south swallowed by the rising silt and vegetation.

For three days he pushed ahead sleeplessly through the forest, feeding on giant berries like clusters of apples, cutting a heavier branch as a crutch. Periodically, to his left, he glimpsed the silver back of a jungle river, its surface dancing in the rain-storms, but massive mangroves formed the banks and he was unable to reach it.

SO HIS DESCENT into the phantasmagoric forest continued, the rain sweeping relentlessly across his face and shoulders. Sometimes it would stop abruptly, and clouds of steam filled the intervals between the trees, hanging over the waterlogged floor like diaphanous fleeces, only dispersing when the downpour resumed.

It was during one of these intermissions that he climbed a steep rise in the centre of a broad clearing, hoping to escape the drenching mists, found himself in a narrow valley between wooded slopes. Crowded with vegetation, the hills rolled around the valley like the dunes he had crossed earlier, enclosing him in a green dripping world. Occasionally, as the mists swirled and lifted, he caught a glimpse of the jungle river between the peaks half a mile away. The wet sky was stained by the setting sun, the pale crimson mists tracing the hill crests in the distance. Pulling himself over the wet clay-like soil, he stumbled into what seemed to be the remains of a small temple. Tilting gate posts led towards a semicircle of shallow steps, where five ruined columns formed a ragged entrance. The roof had collapsed, and only a few feet of the side walls still stood. At the far end of the nave the battered altar looked out over an uninterrupted view of the valley, where the sun sank slowly from sight, its giant orange disc veiled by the mists.

Hoping to shelter there during the night, Kerans walked down the aisle, pausing listlessly as the rain renewed itself. Reaching the altar, he rested his arms on the chest-high marble table, and watched the contracting disc of the sun, its surface stirring rhythmically like the slag on a bowl of molten metal.

'Aaa-ah!' A faint almost inhuman cry sounded thinly into the wet air, like the groan of a stricken animal. Kerans looked around him quickly, wondering if an iguana had followed him into the ruin. But the jungle and the valley and the whole place of stones were silent and motionless, the rain streaming across the cracks in the collapsing walls.

'Aaa-ah!' This time the sound came from in front of him, somewhere towards the fading sun. The disc had pulsed again, apparently drawing forth this strangled response, half in protest, half in gratitude.

Wiping the moisture from his face, Kerans stepped cautiously around the altar, drew back with a start when he almost tripped over the ragged remains of a man sitting with his back to the altar, head propped against the stone. The sounds had obviously come from this emaciated figure, but it was so inert and blackened that Kerans assumed it must be dead.

The man's long legs, like two charred poles of wood, stuck out uselessly in front of him, sheathed in a collection of tattered black rags and bits of bark. His arms and sunken chest were similarly clothed, strung together with short lengths of creeper. A once luxuriant but now thinning black beard covered most of his face, and the rain poured across his hollowed but jutting jaw, which was raised to the fading light. Fitfully the sun shone

on the exposed skin of his face and hands. One of the latter, a
skeletal green claw, suddenly rose like a hand from a grave and
pointed at the sun as if identifying it, then fell limply to the
ground. As the disc pulsed again the face showed some slight
reaction. The deep recesses around the mouth and nose, the hollowed cheeks that encroached so deeply over the broad jaw that
they seemed to leave no space for the buccal cavity within, filled
for a moment as if a single breath of life had passed momentarily
through the body.

Unable to advance, Kerans watched the huge emaciated figure
on the ground before him. The man was no more than a resurrected corpse, without food or equipment, propped against the
altar like someone jerked from his grave and abandoned to await
the Day of Judgement.

Then he realised why the man had failed to notice him.
The dirt and raw sun-blistered skin around the deep eye sockets turned them into blackened funnels, at the base of which a
dull festering gleam reflected faintly the distant sun. Both eyes
were almost completely occluded by corneal cancers, and Kerans
guessed that they would be able to see little more than the dying
sun. As the disc fell away behind the jungle in front of them and
the dusk swept like a pall through the grey rain, the man's head
raised itself painfully, as if trying to retain the image that had
burnt itself so devastatingly upon his retinas, then slumped to
one side against his stone pillow. Flies began to swarm across the
ground and buzzed over his streaming cheeks.

Kerans bent down to speak to the man, who seemed to sense
his movement. Blindly, the hollowed eyes searched the dull nim-
bus beside him.

'Hey, fellow.' His voice was a feeble rasp. 'You there, soldier,
come here! Where have you come from?' His left hand scuttled
around the wet stony clay like a crab, as if looking for something.
Then he turned back to the vanished sun, oblivious of the flies
settling on his face and beard. 'It's gone again! Aa-aah! It's mov-

ing away from me! Help me up, soldier, we'll follow it. Now, before it goes for ever.'

He held his claw out to Kerans, like a dying beggar. Then his head slumped back again and the rain poured over his black skull.

Kerans knelt down. Despite the effects of the sun and rain, the remnants of the man's uniform trousers showed him to be an officer. His right hand, which had remained closed, now opened feebly. In his palm was a small silver cylinder with a circular dial, a pocket compass carried in aircrew rescue kits.

'Hey, soldier!' The man had revived abruptly, his eyeless head turning towards Kerans. 'I order you, don't leave me! You can rest now, while I keep watch. Tomorrow we'll move on.'

Kerans sat down beside him, undid his small parcel and began to wipe the rain and dead flies from the man's face. Taking the ravaged cheeks in his hands like a child's, he said carefully: 'Hardman, this is Kerans—Doctor Kerans. I'll go with you, but try to rest.' Hardman showed no response to the name, his brows creasing slightly in puzzlement.

While Hardman lay back against the altar, Kerans began to dig up some of the cracked flagstones from the aisle with his clasp-knife, carried the pieces back through the rain and built a crude stone shelter around the supine figure, covering the cracks with creeper torn from the walls. Although shielded from the rain, Hardman became slightly restless in the dark alcove, but soon fell into a shallow sleep, now and then breaking into stertorous breaths. Kerans went back through the darkness to the jungle edge, picked an armful of edible berries from the trees, then returned to the shelter and sat beside Hardman until the dawn broke over the hills behind them.

HE STAYED with Hardman for the next three days, feeding him with the berries and spraying his eyes with what was left of the penicillin. He strengthened the hut with more of the flagstones, and built a rough palliasse of leaves for them to sleep on. During the afternoon and evening Hardman would sit in the open door-way, watching the distant sun through the mists. In the intervals between the storms its rain-washed beams lit his green-tinged skin with a strange intense glow. He failed to remember Kerans, and addressed him simply as 'Soldier', sometimes rousing himself from his torpor to issue a series of disconnected orders for the morrow. Increasingly, Kerans felt that Hardman's real personality was now submerged deep within his mind, and that his external behaviour and responses were merely pallid reflections of this, overlayed by his delirium and exposure symptoms. Kerans guessed that his sight had been lost about a month earlier, and that he had crawled instinctively to the higher ground supporting the ruin. From there he could best perceive the sun, the sole entity now strong enough to impinge its image upon his fading retinas.

On the second day Hardman began to eat voraciously, as if preparing himself for another advance through the jungle; by the end of the third day had consumed several bunches of the giant berries. The strength seemed to return suddenly to his great ragged frame, and during the afternoon he managed to support himself on his legs, leaning back against the doorway as the sun sank behind the wooded hills. Whether he now recognised Kerans the latter was unsure, but the monologue of orders and instructions ceased.

Kerans felt little surprise when he woke the next morning and found Hardman had gone. Rousing himself in the thin dawn light, Kerans limped down the valley towards the edge of the forest, where a small stream forked on its way towards the distant river. He looked up at the dark boughs of the fern-trees hanging in the silence. Feebly he shouted Hardman's name, listening to its muted echoes fall away among the sombre trunks, and then returned to the hut. He accepted Hardman's decision to move on without comment, assuming that he might or might not see the man again in the course of their common odyssey southwards.

As long as his eyes were strong enough to sense the distant signals transmitted by the sun, and as long as the iguanas failed
to scent him, Hardman would move forward, feeling his way
through the forest hand over hand, head raised to the sunlight
breaking among the branches.

Kerans waited a further two days at the hut, in case Hardman
chose to return, then set out himself. His medical supplies were
now exhausted, and all he carried was a bag of berries and the
Colt, containing two shells. His watch was still running, and he
used it as a compass, also keeping a careful record of the passage
of the days by notching his belt each morning.

Following the valley, he waded through the shallow stream,
intending to reach the shores of the distant river. Intermittently
heavy rain-storms beat the surface of the water, but these now
seemed concentrated during a few hours in the afternoon and
evening.

When the course of the river required him to move in a west-
erly direction for several miles to reach its banks, he gave up the
attempt and pressed on southwards, leaving the deeper jungle of
the hill region and entering a lighter forest, which in turn gave
way to large tracts of swamp.

Skirting these, he abruptly stepped out on to the shores of an
immense lagoon, over a mile in diameter, ringed by a beach
of white sand, through which protruded the top floors of a few
ruined apartment houses, like beach chalets seen at a distance. In
one of these he rested for a day, trying to mend his ankle, which
had become black and swollen. Looking out from the window at
the disc of water, he watched the afternoon rain discharge itself
into the surface with relentless fury; as the clouds moved away
and the water smoothed itself into a glass sheet its colours seemed
to recapitulate all the changes he had witnessed in his dreams.

That he had travelled over a hundred and fifty miles southward he could tell from the marked rise in temperature. Again
the heat had become all-pervading, rising to a hundred and forty

degrees, and he felt reluctant to leave the lagoon, with its empty beaches and quiet ring of jungle. For some reason he knew that Hardman would soon die, and that his own life might not long survive the massive unbroken jungles to the south.

Half asleep, he lay back thinking of the events of the past years that had culminated in their arrival at the central lagoons and launched him upon his neuronic odyssey, and of Strangman and his insane alligators, and finally, with a deep pang of regret and affection, holding her memory clearly before his mind as long as he could, of Beatrice and her quickening smile.

At last he tied the crutch to his leg again, and with the butt of the empty .45 scratched on the wall below the window, sure that no-one would ever read the message:

27th day. Have rested and am moving south. All is well.
Kerans.

So he left the lagoon and entered the jungle again, within a few days was completely lost, following the lagoons southward through the increasing rain and heat, attacked by alligators and giant bats, a second Adam searching for the forgotten paradises of the reborn sun.

When J.G. Ballard passed in April 2009, the reading world lost one if its most prophetic writers. Over the last century, no other modern fiction writer examined the deleterious effects of technology on culture more unerringly than Ballard, and his surreal, yet richly atmospheric prose has had an indelible effect on Western literature.

Born in Shanghai on November 15, 1930, James Graham Ballard wrote such legendary novels as *The Drowned World* and *Cocaine Nights*, but he is most well-known for *Crash* (1973) and his autobiographical novel *Empire of the Sun* (1984), both of which were made into movies and became box office hits. The author of eighteen novels and twenty short story collections, including *The Complete Short Stories of J.G. Ballard*, which was published to great acclaim in 2009, Ballard has been praised as 'the most original English writer of the last century' (Martin Amis, *The Guardian*) and 'the ideal chronicler of our disturbed modernity' (Jason Cowley, *The Observer*). That his body of work has remained so fresh and shocking makes him a truly unique literary giant, one whose singular imagination will continue to captivate readers for generations to come.